ROAD

TAMBLUFF

BAYBERRY CREEK

HUSTINGREEN

RIVER ROAD

LONG LEAF

LAST CAMP

SINKING CANYONS

RIVER TAM

PINE FLATS

SCOGGIN MOUND

BUG NECK

FEECHIEFEN SWAMP

BEAR HOUSE ISLAND

W9-CKH-507

The Way of the Wilderking

THE WILDERKING TRILOGY

BOOK 3

The Way of the Wilderking

WILDERKING

JONATHAN ROGERS

BROADMAN
& HOLMAN
PUBLISHERS

NASHVILLE, TENNESSEE

© 2006 by Jonathan Rogers
Printed in the United States of America

13-digit ISBN: 978-0-8054-3133-9
10-digit ISBN: 0-8054-3133-0

Published by Broadman & Holman Publishers,
Nashville, Tennessee

Dewey Decimal Classification: F
Subject Headings: ADVENTURE FICTION
                    ADOLESCENCE—FICTION

Interior illustrations by Blake Morgan
Map by Kristi Smith and Blake Morgan

06 07 08 09 10   15 14 13 12 11 10 9 8 7 6 5 4 3 2 1

For my parents,

Delacy and Betsy Rogers

The Wilderking Chant

When fear of God has left the land,
To be replaced by fear of man;
When Corenwalders free and true
Enslave themselves and others too;
When justice and mercy disappear,
When life is cheap and gold is dear,
When freedom's flame has burned to ember
And Corenwalders can't remember
What are truths and what are lies,
Then will the Wilderking arise.

To the palace he comes from forests and swamps.
Watch for the Wilderking!
Leading his troops of wild men and brutes.
Watch for the Wilderking!
He will silence the braggart, ennoble the coward.
Watch for the Wilderking!
Justice will roll, and mercy will toll.
Watch for the Wilderking!
He will guard his dear lambs with the staff of his hand.
Watch for the Wilderking!
With a stone he shall quell the panther fell.
Watch for the Wilderking!

Watch for the Wilderking, widows and orphans.
Look to the swamplands, ye misfit, ye outcast.
From the land's wildest places a wild man will come
To give the land back to her people.

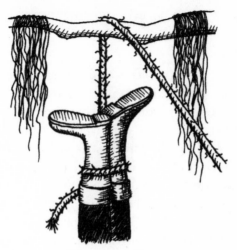

Chapter One

Intruder in the Swamp

A civilizer captured in the Feechiefen. More civilizers on the way with cold-shiny spears and swords and axes and saws. The swamp was abuzz with rumors of new civilizer trouble. When the news reached Bug Neck, Dobro Turtlebane and Aidan Errolson—or Pantherbane, as the feechies knew him—left immediately. They poled all night for Scoggin Mound, where Chief Tombro's feechies held the captured civilizer.

The chill of morning was still on the air when Aidan caught his first glimpse of the towering spruce pines of Scoggin Mound. Well before they could see the island itself, the high, nasally shouts and squeals of a dozen excited wee-feechies carried across the black water to the ears of the two flatboaters.

Then, above the wee-feechies' shrill racket echoed a deeper, prolonged scream—a scream of fear and helplessness. It couldn't have come from a feechie.

It had been three years since Aidan had heard the voice of another civilizer. It had been that long since Aidan had fled the dangers of his civilized life and taken to the swamp to live the life of a feechie. Three years since he had worn anything besides his snakeskin kilt and the panther cape to which he owed his feechie name. Three years since he had eaten from a plate or ridden a horse or been inside a building. With his face and hands daubed with swamp mud, his matted hair draping almost to his shoulders, he hardly looked like a civilizer. He himself had almost forgotten what he was. But something about that throaty howl of human terror—so out of place in the Feechiefen—brought Aidan back to a world he had almost left completely.

With brisker strokes Aidan and Dobro poled for Scoggin Mound. The civilizer's shouts grew even more desperate. "Help me!" he wailed. "Help!" It was a prayer of desperation. And Aidan somehow knew he was the answer to the civilizer's prayer.

The flatboat had scarcely grounded itself before Aidan and Dobro leaped nimbly onto the white sand of the landing at Scoggin Mound. Aidan and Dobro hadn't spoken a word to one another since they first heard the shouts of the wee-feechies, and they didn't speak now as they pounded down the trail toward the ruckus.

2

When Aidan and Dobro crashed through the palmetto and into the clearing, there was already so much commotion that nobody noticed them. It took Aidan a few moments to understand what was going on. A tight knot of wee-feechies was gathered beneath a moss-hung oak tree, arranged in a half circle with their backs to Aidan and Dobro. Though they could hear the civilizer well enough, all Aidan and Dobro could see of him was his boots and black leggings, dangling above the wee-feechies' heads and suspended upside down by a vine rope looped over a branch. A cluster of wee-feechies at the other end of the vine rope raised or lowered their captive by pulling or giving slack.

The screaming of the civilizer was more or less constant, but it grew louder when his tormentors lowered him and less urgent as they raised him. Aidan understood why when he took a step closer. The wee-feechies were gathered around an alligator they had rustled from the swamp—a hungry one by the look of things. It lunged and snapped at the civilizer every time the wee-feechies lowered him, and though the alligator hadn't caught its dinner yet, it wasn't missing by much.

When Dobro understood what the wee-feechies were up to, he was impressed with their ingenuity. "Heh, heh," he chuckled. "Them's some clever rascals." But when he noticed the grim look on Aidan's face, he quickly changed his tune. "Hey, you bumptious scapers!" he yelled at the wee-feechies. "You barbous stinkers, you criminals, you rowdies! Leave that civilizer alone."

"Ooik!" shouted one of the wee-feechies. "It's Pantherbane and Dobro!"

The youngsters scattered, howling with frustration and disappointment. "I don't never get any fun!" one of them complained.

"What I'm supposed to feed my alligator now?" asked another, to nobody in particular.

The wee-feechies who held the rope scattered, too, and when they did, their civilizer thudded to the ground, almost on top of the alligator. Though bound hand and foot, the poor civilizer managed to roll away from the alligator's first lunge. Before it could make a second, Aidan ran up its back and held its jaws shut.

Dobro, meanwhile, was cutting through the vines that tied the civilizer's feet and hands. While he was getting the powerful reptile under control, Aidan could hear Dobro talking to the civilizer.

"You know how younguns is," Dobro was saying. "Always wanting to frolic, always getting into some mischief or other." From the way the civilizer's back was heaving, it appeared he was still gasping for air; in any case, he wasn't answering Dobro. But Dobro didn't seem to notice. "If my remembrance don't mistake me," he continued, "a passel of wee-feechies set old Aunt Seku on Aidan here the first time he come to Scoggin Mound. She 'bout skewered him on the spot."

The civilizer looked over his shoulder at the young man astride the alligator. "Aidan?" the civilizer asked. He nodded in Aidan's direction. "His name's Aidan?"

Aidan was concentrating on the task at hand, but when he heard his name spoken, he looked into the civilizer's face for the first time. His mouth dropped open in astonishment. "Percy!" he shouted, at last recognizing his brother.

Chapter Two

News from the Outside

The two brothers stood staring at one another. Percy knew his brother's voice, and he recognized the broad-shouldered frame shared by all the Errolson brothers. But seeing Aidan in this feechiefied state was disorienting. Percy was sure he had found his brother, and yet he wasn't sure.

The alligator, meanwhile, saw a second chance to get a bite of civilizer, and it meant to take it. It lunged at Aidan, but Dobro picked up a stick left by one of the wee-feechies and brought it down on the alligator's snout, then chased it into the water nearby.

"Aidan?" asked Percy. He rubbed fingers in a circle on Aidan's forehead, trying to get through the swamp mud. "Is that you under there?"

Aidan embraced him. "What are you doing here?"

"Looking for you," Percy answered. "Bringing a warning."

Aidan's eyes narrowed in concern. "What kind of warning?"

"Darrow's army," Percy said. "They left Tambluff a week ago, marching for the Feechiefen."

Dobro had rejoined the conversation by now. "Why you reckon a army of civilizers wants to drown theirselves in the Feechiefen?" he asked.

Percy looked careworn and uncharacteristically somber, older than his twenty-one years. He took a long look at Aidan before he spoke. "It's you they want, Aidan."

Aidan went pale beneath his coating of mud. "Why me?" he asked. "What trouble have I been to King Darrow? Why now? I haven't left this swamp in the last three years." Aidan hadn't even seen the king since the night he'd taken the frog orchid to Tambluff Castle. His hard-won offering was met with the king's implacable hatred and jealousy. Aidan was still a boy then in most ways, a mere fifteen years old. But even then he knew enough to realize his life had changed forever. Rather than provoke further outbursts by the king—and rather than endanger his father and brothers—Aidan had exiled himself to the Feechiefen. There he had stayed ever since, unaware of what was happening in the Corenwald of the civilizers.

"You don't know about the Aidanites, do you?" Percy asked.

"The Aidanites?" Aidan's brow wrinkled in confusion.

Percy took a deep breath. This was going to take some explaining. "The Aidanites," he repeated.

7

"They're your followers. They think they are anyway."

Aidan's head was swimming. "How can I have followers when I'm not leading anybody?"

Percy shrugged. "They call you their king in exile."

Aidan gasped. "I never claimed to be anybody's king!"

Percy's sense of the ridiculous was starting to reassert itself. He couldn't help but chuckle. "Funny, isn't it? In a strange sort of way. The Aidanites go around tacking copies of the Wilderking Chant on trees and buildings all over Corenwald."

Percy launched into the Wilderking Chant:
When fear of God has left the land,
To be replaced by fear of man;
When Corenwalders free and true
Enslave themselves and others too;
When mercy and justice disappear,
When life is cheap and gold is dear,
When freedom's flame has burned to ember
And Corenwalders can't remember
What are truths and what are lies,
Then will the Wilderking arise.

Aidan interrupted the recitation. "Who are these people?"

Percy shrugged. "I don't really know. They operate in secret mostly. I don't know whether there's a dozen of them or a thousand or ten thousand.

But you'd better believe they've got King Darrow wound up."

"Oh no," said Aidan, holding his face in his hands. "Oh no." King Darrow had been insanely, murderously jealous of Aidan when he had no reason to be. What must he be doing now?

"The king has declared us all outlaws," Percy said. "Father, you, me, Brennus, Jasper—Maynard, too, if he ever shows his face in Corenwald again."

Outlaws. The word hit Aidan like a hammer. Their father Errol, one of the Four and Twenty Noblemen of Corenwald, King Darrow's most loyal subject. A magistrate for Hustingshire and the entire Eastern Wilderness, Errol had been the only law between Longleaf Manor and Last Camp, fifty leagues away. Now he and his sons were outside the law's protections; any criminal Errol had ever sent to prison, any jealous rival, any miscreant in Corenwald could commit whatever crime he pleased against Errol or his family, and the law of the land would do nothing about it.

"When did this happen?" asked Aidan.

"About two years ago," his brother answered. "We left Longleaf in the autumn two years ago." Outlaws couldn't own land or pass it on to their heirs, and even if the law allowed it, it wouldn't have been safe to stay. "King Darrow gave our lands to a Fershal from the Hill Country—Lord Fershal, as he's called now. He took Father's place among the Four and Twenty Nobles."

Aidan felt as if the solid ground below him had turned to quicksand. Errol had shaped Longleaf Manor out of pure wilderness. Its lush plantings and spreading meadows, its teeming fishponds and fruit-heavy orchards had been his life's work. The man and the land had survived both drought and flood. Errol had protected his lands from the never-ending encroachment of wilderness—from the weeds and creeping vines that flourished in the rich loam of the floodplain, from the bears, cats, and wolves that carried off his stock. He had defended Longleaf from invading armies, twice rebuilding his house and barns after Pyrthen attackers had burned them to the ground. He had seen five sons born there. There his sweet wife had died when he was still a relatively young man. And now Longleaf Manor, which the armies of Pyrth had never been able to take from Errol or his sons, had been given to a stranger.

When he could speak again, Aidan asked, "So where have you been these two years?"

"We've been at Sinking Canyons most of the time."

Dobro whistled. "Sinking Canyons?" he asked. "About a two days' trot south of Bayberry Swamp?"

"That's right," said Percy. "Down in the Clay Wastes. Do you know it?"

"I reckon I do know it," said Dobro. "All feechie-folks knows about Sinking Canyons. Feechiefolks don't ever go down in it though. Feechiefolks ain't skeered of much, but we good and skeered of holes in the ground." He shuddered. "I peeped over the side of Sinking Canyons once, but you better believe I run off in a hurry. Theto Elbogator told me that hole is still growing, still swallowing up a little more ground every day." He shivered at the thought of it. "Every wee-feechie in the swamp knows a rhyme about Sinking Canyons. Their mamas teach it as a warning to stay away from that place." He began a recitation:

Fallen are the feechiefolks,
In a gully, down a hole.
No more fistfights, no more jokes,
In a gully, down a hole.
To the river, to the woods,
In a gully, down a hole.
Time to leave these neighborhoods.
In a gully, down a hole.

Aidan was getting impatient with this distraction from the matter at hand. He turned back to Percy. "What have you been doing in Sinking Canyons?" he asked. "How do you live there?"

"It's not all that bad," Percy answered. "We live off the land, you might say. Lots of fresh game, berries, roots. Father was able to bring plenty of gold when we left Longleaf, and we send somebody to buy supplies every now and then in Ryelan or Duckington, the nearest villages."

Aidan was growing red in the face. "That's no way for our father to have to live. He's sixty-two years old!"

"You boys is livin' like feechiefolks!" Dobro said. "Living like you got some sense. 'Cept you living in a hole."

Aidan ignored Dobro. He was rolling now, beginning to warm to his subject. "Thrown off his own land! Forced to live in the wilderness!"

Dobro chuckled. "His own land," he mocked. "If you civilizers ain't the beatin'est things. Two civilizers fussing over who owns a piece of land is like two bird lice fussing over who owns the craney-crow."

Aidan gave Dobro a sharp look but didn't say anything. Turning back to his brother, he asked, "Does King Darrow know where you are?"

"Apparently so. He sent a party of six scouts to Sinking Canyons looking for us a couple of years ago. But when they found us, they decided they'd rather stay with us than go back to the army. Darrow sent a second party to find the first party, and they decided to stay too. All twelve of them are still there."

"That must be helpful, having scouts in camp," Aidan observed.

"It has been. They're used to pulling guard duty, and that's freed up the miners to do more tunneling."

"Which miners?"

"The Greasy Cave boys—Gustus, Arliss, and the rest of them—the ones who led you through caverns underneath Bonifay Plain."

"How on earth did they get there?" Aidan asked.

"King Darrow outlawed plenty of people who were associated with you. The Greasy Cave boys, because he thought you were hiding in their mines. The hunters at Last Camp, because they helped you get to the Feechiefen and back when you went after the frog orchid. Lord Aethelbert and Lord Cleland—he had always suspected them of plotting with you when you were at his court. Most of those outlaws have made their way to Sinking Canyons one way or another.

"Then last week one of the Last Campers—Isom, I think it was—went to the village to buy some supplies and came back telling of a new rumor flying around. Folks were saying you had put together an army of feechiefolk in the swamp and were planning to march on Tambluff." He picked up the Wilderking Chant where he had left off a few minutes earlier:

To the palace he comes from forests and swamps.
Watch for the Wilderking!
Leading his troops of wild men and brutes.
Watch for the Wilderking!

"It seems King Darrow wasn't in the mood to watch for the Wilderking any longer," said Percy. "He decided to take the fight to you. He was gathering a force of a thousand men for an invasion of the Feechiefen."

At this news, Dobro perked up. "Invasion? That's a kind of fighting, ain't it?"

Percy sighed. "I'm afraid so, Dobro."

Dobro jumped up and clapped his heels together. "Hee-haw!" he yodeled. "What some fun! I ain't done no serious fighting since the Battle of Bearhouse!"

"No!" Aidan groaned. "They can't come to the Feechiefen!"

"Let's see here," said Dobro, more to himself than to his companions. "A thousand civilizers"—he was scratching in the sand with a stick—"if every feechie whips about fifty civilizers . . ."

"They're staging from Last Camp," said Percy. "They'll be ferrying men across the Tam from there."

Dobro gave up scratching in the sand. "I never learnt no number figuring," he said, "but I don't reckon a thousand civilizers is near enough to go around."

"We can't let a civilizer army come into the Feechiefen," Aidan said. "They'd never survive here."

Percy nodded in agreement. "Father sent me to warn you and the feechiefolk. Now I see you aren't the ones who need warning. It's Darrow's soldiers who are in real danger."

"You reckon there's any way the king'd bring more'n a thousand fighting men?" Dobro interrupted. "A thousand civilizers ain't hardly worth poling across the swamp for."

Chapter Three

Timberbout

By midafternoon, three dozen or more feechies, attracted by the news of the captured civilizer, arrived at Scoggin Mound from all over the swamp. They represented eight different bands, enough to form a swamp council.

As home chieftain, Tombro Timberbeaver led the proceedings. He climbed a stump in the middle of the central clearing, near the village fire, and raised a hand for silence among the gathered feechies. When that didn't work (raising a hand for silence almost never worked with feechies), he simply shouted over everyone. "Let this here swamp council come to order!" he bellowed. "Or if that's too much to ask, let this here swamp council come to a little less disorder."

The noise died down the least little bit, and Tombro began. "First off, let me say sorry to Percy. We didn't know you was Pantherbane's brother." He nodded toward Percy. "We thought you was a spy."

"He told you he wasn't a spy, didn't he?" asked Aidan.

"Well, yeah," said Tombro. "But I ain't exactly in the habit of listening to what civilizers says."

"Besides," said Hyko Vinesturgeon, "ain't that what a real spy would say? No spy worth the name gonna tell you he's a spy."

"What kind of spy comes to warn you that his own army is planning an invasion?" Aidan asked.

"We just figured he was bragging," Tombro answered, a little weakly.

"Didn't he tell you he was my brother?" Aidan asked.

"Sorta yes, sorta no," Tombro said.

Percy had been quiet thus far, but this answer got under his skin. "Sorta yes? I must have told you a hundred times I was Aidan Errolson's brother."

"Well, that's the thing," said Tombro. "I don't know nothing about no Aidan Errolson. Now Pantherbane—I'd swim nekkid through a herd of snapping turtles for Pantherbane or any of his folks."

"Nobody around here knows my civilizer name," Aidan explained to his brother. "All they know is Pantherbane."

"Oh, and about what them wee-feechies done to you, Percy—about them feeding you to that alligator." Tombro was trying to keep a grave and apologetic face, but something twinkled in his eye. Was it pride in the wee-feechies' spirit and creativity? "They ought notta done that." The wee-feechies had sneaked Percy out of his cage while the grown-ups were embroiled in a heated argument over what they should do to him. "But you know how younguns is," Tombro concluded. It wasn't the most satisfying apology Percy had ever received.

"Say, Tombro," Aunt Seku called. "Ain't you forgettin' somethin'?"

"I didn't pole half a day just for jabbering and sorrifyin'," said one of the Coonhouse feechies. "You want to confabulate about this here civilizer trouble, that's fine with me. But looks to me like you owe me some entertainment first."

A murmur of agreement rippled through the assembled feechies. Orlo Polejumble called out, "Tombro, I want to see can't Wimbo Barkflinger whup your daddy's beavers at long last."

Percy was confused, being unfamiliar with feechie ways. Wasn't this an emergency swamp council? What did entertainment have to do with anything? But Aidan just groaned. A timber-cutting contest would mean at least an hour's delay, and they didn't have an hour to spare.

"The civilizers are coming!" Aidan shouted, trying to make himself heard. "We don't have time—"

But his voice was drowned out by a rising chant: "Timberbout! Timberbout! Timberbout!"

The crowd pushed Wimbo Barkflinger and Bardo Timberbeaver, Tombro's father, toward the stump in the middle of the clearing. Wimbo looked uncertain about going up against Bardo's beavers, but Bardo rubbed his hands in evident glee. Wimbo was the greatest of the Feechiefen axmen. No man alive could outchop him with a stone ax. But nobody, not even Wimbo, had ever beaten Bardo's team of trained beavers in a timberbout. The Timberbeaver clan derived its name from these very creatures, so great was the clan's pride in them.

Wimbo raised his palms in front of his face, the backs of his hands facing outward. It was the gesture by which a feechie accepts a public challenge. The crowd grew silent.

"Bardo, I'll chop against your beavers," he said, "on one condition." The beaver trainer inclined his head toward the timber cutter and smiled, inviting him to name his condition.

"Let me pick out the trees," Wimbo said.

Bardo shrugged. "I don't see what difference that makes, long as the trees is the same kind and about the same size." That was a given anyway, according to the rules of a timberbout. "And as long as you don't pick out pine trees. You know my beavers can't abide pitch and turpentine. It ain't natural."

Wimbo agreed and butted heads with the old feechie to seal the deal.

"Well then," said Bardo, "I better go fetch my beavers." The crowd cheered in raucous anticipation of the timberbout, and the feechies all fell in behind Bardo as he stomped down the trail toward the landing.

Near the water's edge, Bardo found the cypress paddle he used to call his beavers. He slapped it flat on the surface of the water, in imitation of a beaver's tail slapping. *Slap! Slap! Slap-slap-slap! Slap! Slap! Slap-slap-slap!* It wasn't long before three deep-brown knobs appeared on the black water's surface, approaching fast and trailing broadening Vs in their wake.

"Hyah, Sawtooth!" Bardo called. "Hyah, Crackjaw! Hyah, Chip!"

The three massive, glistening, dripping beavers emerged from the swamp and waddled briskly to Bardo, then sat on their haunches in affectionate greeting to the old feechie who had raised them from kits and trained them in the finer points of competitive tree felling.

"There's my thunder beavers," Bardo crooned, stroking each in turn. "There's my trunk snappers." The beavers arched their backs in pleasure at their master's praise. "I got 'em when they was wee fellers, and I raised 'em into tree fellers," Bardo cackled. In spite of his impatience with the whole situation, Aidan couldn't help but be warmed by the obvious affection between the wrinkled old feechie and his furry friends.

It was comical to see such heavy creatures frisk about in their lubberly way. Even so, there was something nervous and high-strung in the beavers' manner. Bardo bred his beavers to be energetic and competitive, and while beavers were proverbially eager, these particular beavers went beyond eager to something more like manic. From the moment they got out of the water, they worked their powerful jaws, flashing their huge front cutting teeth as if they couldn't wait to start gnawing something.

"Pick your trees, Wimbo," said Bardo, "before Sawtooth commences to chawin' up somebody's leg."

Wimbo looked around at the nearby trees. His gaze soon fell on a pair of nearly identical loblolly bays, each about a foot in diameter, standing some ten strides apart. "How 'bout them two trees?" he suggested.

"My beavers thinks a bay tree's a stick of sugar cane," Bardo boasted. "I imagine they ate two or three for breakfast this morning. You sure you don't want to try your luck on somethin' a little more challengin'?"

"Naw," Wimbo answered. He had already unslung the hickory-handled stone ax he always carried on his back and was scraping himself a footpad in the sand at the base of one of the bays. "I reckon these two trees will serve."

"All right then," Bardo answered, herding his beavers toward the second bay tree. "Circle up, Sawtooth! Circle up, Chip! Crackjaw!"

The three beavers circled around their tree, and it was all Bardo could do to keep them from tearing into the bark before Tombro gave the start whistle.

When Tombro's whistle shrilled across the little island, Wimbo Barkflinger fell to with all the passion and determination of wounded pride. Bardo's beavers had bested him in ten straight contests. They were the bane of his existence. He strained every muscle and sinew, he rotated at the hips, he kept his feet planted. And the chips rained in a steady shower.

The beavers, however, weren't making nearly so much progress. They attacked their tree with all the enthusiasm their master had bred and trained into them. But they quickly fell back like soldiers repulsed by an enemy.

"Have at it, my champeens!" Bardo urged. "Fling bark! Grind that tree! Chop it!"

At Bardo's encouragement the beavers launched a second attack. But it was no good. They each made no more than a superficial scrape in the tree's bark before they went to sneezing and coughing. They curled up their lips and wrinkled their noses so their front teeth protruded even more, a grotesque exaggeration of a beaver's already ludicrous profile.

Meanwhile, Wimbo chopped away, seemingly unaware of the big lead he was gaining on his opponents.

"At it, my darlings!" Bardo urged. "Make stumps, my princes!" But by this time, the beavers were rooting like hogs, snorting and sneezing in the sand at the tree's base.

"What's a matter with them beavers?" somebody asked from the crowd.

Bardo got on his hands and knees, the better to coax along his three champions. That's when he noticed little balls of pine resin in Crackjaw's whiskers. Examining his beavers' tree—the tree Wimbo had selected for them to gnaw—Bardo realized it had been painted all the way around with turpentine and resin. Bardo's eyes were flashing when he turned them on Wimbo, still swinging away at his own bay tree.

It didn't take Bardo long to figure out what had happened. Wimbo must have known he would be called on to compete against Bardo's beavers once again. He had to have known. Every time he came to the Timberbeavers' home island, somebody urged a timberbout on him. Wimbo, the rascal, had painted this tree with turpentine and pine resin after he arrived the night before. No wonder the wily axman had insisted he be allowed to select the trees himself. Bardo looked at his unhappy beavers who, at his urging, had taken two mouthfuls of turpentine. Looking at Wimbo's flailing form, fury rose like a red mist before Bardo's eyes. He pointed his cypress paddle at the axman. "Hyah, Sawtooth! Hyah, Crackjaw! Hyah, Chip!" he intoned. "Chaw him!"

In a feat of athleticism unheard of among beavers, one of Bardo's darlings—Chip, Bardo later said—jumped three feet off the sand and hit Wimbo square in the belly while the axman was on the backswing. Wimbo went down in a heap, covering himself against the flashing teeth of his attacker. Sawtooth went to work on his shinbone while Crackjaw made short work of the hickory handle on Wimbo's ax.

When Crackjaw had destroyed Wimbo's ax, Bardo called his beavers off Wimbo and set them on Wimbo's tree. The Feechiefen's greatest axman just watched as the three beavers finished the job he had started. The gathered feechies scattered as the tree thundered to earth. Wimbo had been handed his eleventh straight defeat in a timberbout.

Chapter Four

Swamp Council

The muddy faces of the swamp councilors were still alight with the excitement of the timberbout when Tombro called the meeting to order a second time.

"A thousand civilizers," Tombro began, "crossing the river and coming this way. What you reckon we ought to do 'bout it?"

"Whup 'em!" shouted Theto Elbogator. He shook his fist ominously.

"Drown 'em!" offered an ill-favored she-feechie from Turtle Strand.

"What are we waitin' for?" whooped a pinch-faced member of Larbo's band whom Aidan recognized from the Battle of Bearhouse. He raised a spear above his head, holding it with both hands, and ran a lap around the gathering, trying to whip his fellows into a warlike frenzy.

On the warmonger's second pass, Tombro grabbed hold of his spear and wrenched it from his hands. "Hold on, Sligo," Tombro said. "The time'll come for whuppin', but now's the time for talkin'." He turned toward Aidan. "Pantherbane, you a civilizer—used to be anyway. What you think about all this?"

Aidan was slow to answer. "The thought of civilizers in the Feechiefen scares me to death," he finally said.

The gathered feechies breathed a collective gasp.

"Bless him," said Aunt Seku. "He's scared of civilizers."

"Don't you worry about a thing, Pantherbane," Branko Flatbottom called. "We won't let them mean old civilizers catch you. Your fights is our fights, remember?"

"No," said Aidan, "it's not that. I'm afraid that if a thousand civilizer soldiers came into the Feechiefen, they'd never go home alive."

"Hee-haw!" yodeled one of the feechies.

"That'll learn 'em!" shouted another.

But it was plain neither Aidan nor Percy took any pleasure in the idea.

"What you boys mullygrubbin' for?" Dobro asked. "Surely it don't hurt your feelin's none to see your enemies whupped?"

Aidan shook his head. "Those soldiers aren't my enemies . . . even if they think they are."

Dobro snorted. "I don't believe you know what a enemy is."

Percy spoke now. His tone was unusually solemn. "About a quarter of those fighting men are from the Hustingreen Regiment. Some of them probably worked on our farm in harvesttime. We saw them on market days, played with them on the ferry landing when we were boys."

"They aren't our enemies," Aidan repeated. "They're our countrymen. And they're just following orders."

"Follerin' orders?" Dobro barked. "How 'bout the feller what gave the orders? Is he a enemy or not?"

It was a good question. Aidan, like his brothers and his father, had pledged allegiance to King Darrow. But that was before Darrow had turned on Aidan, before he had run Aidan's family off its land. Was Darrow his king or his enemy? For years now, Aidan had been able to put the question out of his mind. He had been happy in the swamp and far beyond King Darrow's reach or influence. In the Feechiefen he hadn't needed to have an opinion about King Darrow. He didn't have to be a friend or an enemy. But now it was clear: He would soon have to decide.

Dobro was in Aidan's face now, poking a finger in his chest. Aidan could feel his old friend's rancid breath on his cheek. "I asked you a question, Aidan Pantherbane. Is King Darrow your enemy or not?"

Aidan looked to Percy, but his brother wouldn't meet his gaze. Aidan shoved Dobro back out of his face. "I don't know, Dobro," he said. "I don't know yet."

In the silence that followed, Aidan understood what he had to do—at least part of what he had to do. "Those civilizers won't make it to the Feechiefen," he announced. "I'll see to that myself." All around him, eyes narrowed as the feechies tried to understand what he meant.

"Pantherbane, I don't mean no disrespect, and we all know you got what it takes," Tombro began. "But ain't a thousand civilizers with cold-shiny arms more'n you can handle? Even if your brother helps you?"

"No, listen here," Aidan said. "If I leave the Feechiefen—and if King Darrow knows it—he'll never send his men into the swamp." Aidan took a deep breath before he spoke the next sentence. "I'm leaving the Feechiefen. Right now."

The gasps of fifty feechiefolk sounded like the rustle of leaves before a thunderstorm.

"Aidan," said Tombro, "we can hide you as long as you want to be hid, and your brother too. And if you don't want us whuppin' your civilizer friends, or enemies, whatever they are"—here he looked around nervously, not sure if his fellows would agree—"I reckon we could resist it."

"Thank you, Tombro," said Aidan, "but I won't ask you to do that. If civilizers come into Feechiefen, there's bound to be bad trouble. And even if you didn't whip them, the alligators and the wolves and the quicksand would.

"No," he continued, "every hour I stay here, I'm putting the peace of this whole swamp in danger. And I'm putting those thousand civilizer soldiers in danger—and the five thousand King Darrow will send when they're gone, and the ten thousand he'll send after that."

"But, Pantherbane," came the piping voice of a wee-feechie who had sneaked into the swamp council. "You gonna come back, ain't you?"

"No, Betsu," Aidan answered, "I don't reckon I ever will."

The stunned silence in the clearing was broken by a wave of wailing lamentations. Percy was astonished to see half the feechiefolk wallowing in the sand for sorrow at Aidan's departure.

Aidan couldn't bear the thought of saying good-bye to the people who had been his gracious hosts and faithful friends these three years. He knew if he didn't slip away immediately, somebody would start organizing a farewell feast in his honor, complete with fistfights and feechiesings and probably a gator grabble. He just didn't have the time. He grabbed Percy by the elbow, and the two brothers disappeared into the forest.

Running for the north end of Scoggin Mound, Aidan heard the slightest rustle in the treetops, and he realized he and Percy were not alone. "Dobro?" he called. "Is that you?"

"It's me," came the answer from somewhere in the treetop.

"Go back, Dobro. We're going to civilizer country."

Dobro slid down a vine and dropped to the ground beside them. "I know," he said. "I been thinkin' I might take up civilizin' my own self. Maybe get me a horse to ride around on, marry me one of them pretty civilizer gals, and raise some civilizer younguns."

Aidan couldn't help but smile at the thought. But he knew the swamp was the place for Dobro. "No, I think this is good-bye, friend. Maybe we can meet at the Bear Trail one of these new moons. But you'd better get back to the swamp council. Tell everybody good-bye for me."

"I don't reckon I will," said Dobro, in a very matter-of-fact tone. "And I don't reckon you could make me. I'm comin' with you."

Aidan didn't have time to argue. "Maybe you could escort us as far as Big Bend."

"Sure, I'll escort you to Big Bend," said Dobro. "Then I'm gonna escort you across the river, and I'm gonna escort you wherever you go in civilizer country, and me and your brothers is gonna be big buddies, and your daddy's gonna treat me like his own son. Your fights is my fights, Aidan."

Dobro among civilizers. Aidan didn't see any way it could work. It had disaster written all over it. He had to think of something, and fast. So he lied. "Here's the thing, Dobro. I don't want you to come with me."

Dobro just shrugged. "Want me or don't want me. It don't make me no never mind. I'm comin' with you."

Aidan looked at Dobro and sighed. He was one determined feechie. And the truest friend in the world. In truth, Aidan couldn't bear the thought of parting ways with Dobro, whatever trouble he might cause among the civilizers.

"Come on, then," he said.

"Haw-wee!" Dobro whooped, and he put one arm around Aidan's neck and the other around Percy's. "Let's go get civilized!"

Chapter Five

To the Tam

Percy, Dobro, and Aidan traveled north from Scoggin Mound by flatboat, then through the treetops. Percy, like his brother, proved a natural tree-walker, swinging and leaping with the easy rhythm of the feechiefolks. They saw neither soldiers nor signs of soldiers in the Feechiefen, in the bordering scrub swamp, or in the pine flats beyond. However, when they made it to the River Tam around dusk on the second day of their travels, it became clear they had nearly waited too long.

On the south bank of the river—the feechie bank—five soldiers from King Darrow's army were guarding a huge mound of supplies ferried over that day. In the failing light, Aidan could make out bundle upon bundle of steel-tipped arrows, piles of timber axes, two bales of extra uniforms, and stacks of shovels. A string of pack mules stamped and twitched nervously, seemingly aware that they didn't belong on this side of the River Tam. The civilizer guards looked skittish themselves. From their perch in the tree directly above, Percy, Dobro, and Aidan could hear every word they said.

"Look at them cooking fires," one of the soldiers said. Across the river, fifty fires flickered beneath the sheltering trees of Last Camp. "They look cheerful from here, don't they?"

"Earl, everything looks cheerful compared to this place," said one of the others. "It feels like this forest is gonna swallow us whole. We got no business over here." The pitch of his voice rose with that last sentence.

"Keep your leggings on, Hadley," said a third soldier. "Things'll look a whole lot better tomorrow morning when the rest of the force crosses over."

Hadley wasn't satisfied. "You reckon we'll even see tomorrow morning? I'm telling you, this place gives me the fantods. Ain't nobody ever come back from this side of the river, Wat."

"Ain't nobody ever come a thousand men at a time," Wat answered.

"I don't know. It might be just nine hundred and ninety-five by morning."

"Hush that talk, Luther," said Earl. "You're as bad

as Hadley. Besides," he added, "Aidan Errolson came back alive once."

"Aidan Errolson!" a fifth soldier said. "I 'bout had a bellyful of Aidan Errolson. Weren't for Aidan Errolson, I'd be home where I belong, mowing hay for my cattle, dandling my new baby on my lap in the evenings."

"It ain't Aidan Errolson's fault you ain't home on the farm, Cordel," said Luther. "That was King Darrow's idea."

"I don't care whose idea it was," said Hadley. "We got no business this side of the river. The thousand of us ain't going to catch him, even if he's still alive— which I doubt."

"We couldn't catch him in the Feechiefen even if there was a *hundred* thousand of us," Cordel agreed. "Even if all hundred thousand of us actually wanted to catch him."

"What's that supposed to mean?" Luther asked. "You don't want to catch him?"

"Aidan Errolson can go about his business, as far as I'm concerned," said Cordel. "If I can just go about mine. I got hay in the field, and I got a baby needs dandling, and if King Darrow got a beef with Aidan Errolson, I wish he'd leave me out of it!"

"Seems to me," said Earl, "a fellow plans to invade my country, burn my crops, carry off my children, he deserves what he gets. King Darrow's right, we ought to be taking the fight to him before he overruns all of civilization with a crowd of stinking feechies."

"Feechies!" Wat scoffed. "Feechies! This ain't play nursery, Earl. Why you telling nursery stories?"

"What?" asked Earl. "You don't believe the Feechiefen's full of feechies?"

Wat snorted. "Only thing full of feechies is the minds of babies and half-wits. Feechies! It's all hokey-pokey. It's all oogey-boogey."

Dobro couldn't possibly resist such an invitation. He sailed from his perch in the tree and landed on the bale of uniforms where Wat was sitting. Then he flipped over Wat's head and landed on the ground in the middle of the soldiers. "Hokey-pokey!" he yelled. "Oogey-boogey!" He whirled around the civilizers like a dust devil, his arms gyrating, his long hair flapping behind him, roaring and yodeling. Then he jumped on Wat's back and rode the poor civilizer until he tripped over a cypress knee and planted himself in the mud. The rest of the soldiers scattered into Tamside Forest.

Aidan and Percy, meanwhile, scrambled down the tree and climbed down the riverbank into a little rowboat that floated in the eddy. In a matter of seconds, Dobro sailed from the bank and into the boat in a single catlike leap.

Percy nearly had the mooring rope loose when Aidan yelled, "Wait!" and scrambled up the root tangle and disappeared over the bank again. He returned in no time and jumped back into the boat. "Here," he said, handing each of his companions a blue tunic he pulled from the uniform bale. "We might need these."

Percy rowed the boat a quarter league down-stream, well beyond the last of the civilizers' dying cooking fires, before rowing across to the north side, where they beached their craft on a sandbar.

"Home again, home again," Percy said softly. He seemed genuinely relieved to be back on the civilizer side of the river, in spite of the danger.

Aidan's feelings weren't so straightforward. He was born and bred in civilizer country. He had spent fifteen of his eighteen years there, most of them happy. But the Feechiefen had begun to feel like home. It certainly felt like sanctuary.

Dobro, of course, had been to the civilizer side of the river before, but he had always stayed in the forests and swamps. Soon he would get his first taste of actual civilization.

Aidan stood in the river and squatted to wet himself all over. He grabbed a handful of sand and scoured his bare chest, back, legs, and face. A cloud of gray swamp mud—a feechie's protective coating against bugs and sunburn—spread in the water around him and drifted downstream toward the Eastern Ocean.

"Come on, Dobro," Aidan said. "It's time for you to get cleaned up."

Dobro took a step back, away from the water. "I don't believe I will," he said. "I done made it eighteen years without getting bathified, and I don't reckon I'll start now."

"Come on, Dobro," Aidan repeated. "You can't get civilized if you're covered in mud."

"How's that civilized," Dobro asked, "to walk around all pink and shiny? Like a boiled crawfish? Naw, I'd sooner walk around nekkid."

Percy joined in. "How do you figure to get a civilizer girl to marry you if you smell like swamp rot and look like a lizard?"

Dobro crossed his arms and looked just over Percy's head with an air of exaggerated dignity. "Any gal don't love me for my own self, she ain't worthy of me."

Aidan's tone betrayed his exasperation. "Dobro, we don't have many hours before sunup. The camp will be waking soon, and then they'll start crossing the river into feechie country. There's the rowboat. You're welcome to it if you want to go home. But if you want to come with us, get over here and let me wash you off."

Dobro walked slowly toward the water, holding his head down and looking at Aidan through his eyebrows. He put one toe in the water, testing it. This, the same Dobro who thought nothing of diving into the black, alligator-infested waters of the Feechiefen in pursuit of a muskrat. "Ooh!" he moaned. "It's wet!"

Growing impatient, Aidan grabbed Dobro by the arm and dunked him in the water. "Help!" Dobro spluttered, flailing the water to a froth. "He's drownin' me!"

When Aidan began scouring Dobro's muddy back with sand, the feechie wailed like a wounded animal.

"Awww! Awww! He's skinnin' me alive! I'm ruint! Awww! Leave a little skin on me, you cannibal! You monster!"

"S-s-s-h-h-h!" Aidan hissed. "If you don't get quiet, a thousand civilizers are going to be down here to watch you bathe."

"Nine hundred and ninety-five," Percy corrected.

Dobro finally got quiet. Dripping and sulking, he had the look of a cat forced to submit to a bath at the hands of a child. Aidan finished the job in short order. Dobro, it turned out, was shockingly white under all that mud; his skin had never been exposed directly to the sun, after all. He looked like a second moon, like a creature made to be camouflaged on a sandbar. Aidan wondered if he would ever get used to a Dobro who wasn't gray skinned. Dobro, for his part, looked mournfully at his arms and legs, as if they were the limbs of a foreigner.

When baths were finished, Aidan fetched his side pouch from the sandbar and pulled out his prized possession, the steel hunting knife he had hidden there three years earlier. Out of respect for the feechies' aversion to cold-shiny implements and weapons, he had never used it in the swamp; he had pulled it out only to clean and sharpen it every month or so. But now that he was back on the civilizer side of the river, he was glad to see it again. He handed the knife to Percy and pointed to the hair that draped down the back of his own neck. "Cut it off, Percy," he said. "Make it look like civilizer hair."

Dobro sobbed quietly while Percy performed the same operation on his hair—his "mane" as he-feechies liked to call it. When the Errolsons weren't looking, Dobro picked up a matted hank of his hair and put it in his side pouch, a memento of the life he had left behind.

The three travelers all donned blue army tunics; Aidan and Dobro wore theirs over their snakeskin kilts. Only Percy's disguise was halfway convincing, since Aidan and Dobro had neither leggings nor boots. Even by moonlight it was clear Dobro wouldn't pass for a civilizer in the daylight. But he was a little less feechiefied, and for the time being that would have to do.

Leaving the sandbar, Percy, Aidan, and Dobro entered the forest and tree-walked upstream, with the river on their left. Some thirty feet above the ground, they traversed Last Camp, where nine hundred ninety-five soldiers slept their last few hours before stepping off the edge of civilization and into the unknown—or so they thought.

The cooking fires had all burned to ashes, and from such a height, Aidan, Dobro, and Percy could see very little. But as they passed over the center of Last Camp, Aidan saw the least glimmer of gold embroidery catch the moonlight; he knew it could only be the battle standard of King Darrow himself, the golden boar under which King Darrow led his troops. It almost made Aidan dizzy to think of his king down there, so far below him—and dreaming of what? Was he dreaming of Aidan's destruction?

The three travelers hurried across the treetops, in only a few minutes coming to the Overland Trail that led to River Road. Alighting on the ground, they agreed to hide in the forest and sleep until daylight. They would need to be as rested and as clearheaded as possible when the army awoke in a couple of hours.

Both Percy and Dobro were breathing heavily and slowly mere seconds after lying on the moss bed they had found. But Aidan couldn't sleep for thinking about the king who slept just a few hundred yards away. He quietly arose and shinned up a nearby tree. He swung and leaped from limb to limb until he was back at the center of Last Camp. He slunk to the lowest branch of the tree under which King Darrow slept. He could hear his king snoring.

Sitting on that limb, Aidan thought over what Dobro had said earlier: "I don't think you know what a enemy is." It was time he decided: Was King Darrow his enemy, or wasn't he?

The morning star was rising. The camp would probably be up and stirring in half an hour, maybe even less. Aidan made his decision. He pulled the hunting knife out of his side pouch, clenched the blade in his teeth pirate fashion, and descended as stealthily as a panther toward the sleeping king.

Chapter Six

Last Camp

The bodyguards surrounding King Darrow faced outward, their backs to the king, the better to confront whatever danger might come from any point of the compass. It never occurred to anyone that danger might come from directly above. King Darrow stirred when Aidan touched down in the sand beside him. But the guards heard nothing and did not see the knife-wielding phantom who stood over the man they had sworn to protect.

Darrow stirred again when Aidan's cold blade touched his collarbone. But Aidan was sure of his purpose and unflinching in its execution. He lifted the leather strap that rested against King Darrow's neck. When the king was in Tambluff Castle, he wore a medallion of a golden boar, his badge of kingship, on a thick chain of gold. Here in the field, the badge of kingship hung from this leather strap around his neck. Aidan cut it with a single swipe of his knife. As deftly as any thief, he palmed the medallion and dropped it in his side pouch. Then he shinned back up the tree trunk before being noticed by either Darrow or his guards.

Aidan hadn't been back in his treetop perch five minutes when the river mists that covered Last Camp lightened from gray to white in the first rays of dawn. The camp came to life in the morning light. The men were making their final preparations, checking their gear one last time before lining up to cross on the ferries. No one relit the cooking fires. No time for breakfast on such a day as this. The men drank water from their canteens and gnawed stale flatbread, not even sitting down to eat.

King Darrow was up with the rest of the men. He had been a warrior even longer than he had been a king, and he wasn't one to lie about while a campaign was afoot. His hair had gone almost completely white in the years since Aidan had last seen him. That was a shock to Aidan, though perhaps it shouldn't have been; the king was nearly seventy years old. Nor did King Darrow still move with the manly grace of his younger years. A night sleeping unsheltered on the ground had left him stiff in his joints. He was too old to be leading a military expedition into the Feechiefen Swamp. He was too old to nurse the sort of grudge that would drive him to do such a thing. But there he was, giving orders, hearing reports from lieutenants, pointing at maps.

Darrow was leaning over to tighten a boot lace when he noticed that his badge of kingship was missing. He clutched at the ends of the severed strap that hung loose about his neck. Aidan watched as the king patted around his chest and belly for any sign of the missing medallion. But even as he did so, it was obvious that King Darrow understood the truth: His badge of kingship had been taken.

"My badge of kingship!" King Darrow bellowed, and his voice echoed all the way across to the feechie side of the River Tam. "My badge of kingship! Who has stolen my kingship from me?"

The faces of the four night bodyguards were ashen. Their terror was plain to see. Darrow snatched the strap from around his neck and used it as a whip to lash his bodyguards about the head and shoulders. "My kingship!" he roared. "Someone has stolen my kingship from me!" The guards made no move to protect themselves from the lashing but stood erect and looked straight ahead, absorbing this abuse from the king.

Throughout the camp, all preparations for the crossing stopped as men gaped at the king's outburst. Darrow was still roaring and flailing like a crazy man when a tall, dark-haired young man strode up behind him. In his bearing was all the natural command of a man born to rule. He was the very picture of King Darrow when he was younger, when he still had all his wits about him. "Father," he said firmly but gently. He put a comforting hand on the older man's shoulder. "Father, no one has taken your kingship from you."

King Darrow let the strap fall to the ground. The presence of his son Steren brought him back to himself. Aidan, too, was moved by the sight of his dearest friend in all the civilized world. The mere sight of Steren—the true, the brave, the just Steren—awakened in Aidan a loyalty that had lain dormant during his years in the swamp. Steren stood for all that was good about Corenwalder civilization. Aidan could see in the soldiers' faces a love for the prince that far outstripped any love they still had for his father the king.

"No one has taken your kingship from you," Steren repeated, "but your *badge* of kingship—I will not rest until it has been returned to you." He fixed his gray eyes on the bodyguards, convinced that at least one of them knew something of the medallion's whereabouts. The bodyguards, who had stood so bravely under the king's lashing, wilted under the prince's glare.

The long silence that followed was broken by a clear voice in the tree limbs high above the bodyguards' heads. "Your Majesty," the voice called. King Darrow, Prince Steren, and nine hundred ninety-five Corenwalder soldiers squinted to see Aidan Errolson dangling the badge of kingship from the tip of a hunting knife. The four bodyguards, anxious to make up for their earlier negligence, lifted crossbows to shoot Aidan out of the tree, but Steren raised a restraining hand.

Those soldiers who had been conscripted from Hustingreen knew Aidan by sight, and the whispered news raced around Last Camp: The man they were going to seek had come instead to them.

Aidan bowed in the direction of King Darrow. "Your badge of kingship." He flipped the medallion toward the nearest bodyguard, who dropped his crossbow in order to catch it. "With all the glad heart of a loyal subject, I return it to my king." After three years among the plain-spoken feechies, such courtly language no longer came naturally to Aidan. But the assembled soldiers seemed to think it a pretty sentiment. They appeared to be on the verge of applauding Aidan.

King Darrow, for his part, was speechless with rage. Nor did Steren look very pleased with his old friend's gesture. "A loyal subject," Steren said in clipped tones, "would not have stolen from his sovereign to begin with."

Some of Aidan's self-satisfaction ebbed away under the stern gaze of the crown prince. "I truly meant it as a gesture of goodwill," Aidan said, not quite so confidently. "To show His Majesty, and every man assembled here, that I would never do my king harm."

The king's rage boiled over at this. "You lie!" he shouted. "You have done me many harms! The subjects whose loyalty you have stolen—"

"Your Majesty, I would never—"

"The swamp men you have organized into a hostile army—"

"No, Your Majesty—"

"My own son, whom you almost turned against me . . ." As if it weakened him merely to speak of such things, the king leaned heavily on Steren, who neither frowned nor smiled at Aidan.

Aidan extended the hand that held the hunting knife. "This morning I held this knife an inch away from Your Majesty's throat, while you slept." His hand shook as he spoke, and his voice trembled. "If I had meant you any harm, I could have done you harm."

This statement seemed to get through to the king, whose aspect softened, though only a little. Aidan continued. "I'm about to go away. Pursue me if you must. But I make this solemn promise: I will not cross again into the land of the feechiefolk. You need not look for me there."

King Darrow snorted. "Why should I believe that?"

"Because I have never lied to you."

In that moment King Darrow understood Aidan was telling the truth, as he always had. "Why would you make me such a promise?" the king asked.

"Because I am not worth the lives of a thousand men. If you lead these men into the Feechiefen, you will be leading them to their deaths. The feechies are fierce, and they aren't forgiving of outsiders who invade their swamp."

Aidan paused to let the king and his men think about what he had said. "I will run for my life if I have to, Your Majesty. But you have my word: I won't run that way."

King Darrow pondered Aidan's promise. Something about it rankled him—the quarry defining the terms of the chase. Years of smoldering hatred got the better of him. "I will end this now!" he announced. "Archers!"

Fifty archers raised their bows and awaited the distasteful order from their king—to shoot Aidan Errolson down like a roosting bird. But Prince Steren intervened again. "Wait, Father—Your Majesty," he called. "There is a more honorable way. I will end this myself." The look he fixed on Aidan was grim.

Among the king's many jealousies was Darrow's jealousy of Aidan's friendship with his son. It pleased Darrow to see Steren taking his side in this conflict. He motioned to the archers to stand down. Steren kicked off his boots and checked to be sure his knife was in its sheath. Aidan watched in mute astonishment, his feet rooted to the limb on which he stood, while Steren climbed swiftly, feechielike, toward him.

Aidan had faced down alligators and wolves, a giant and a rattlesnake, the Pyrthens' thunder-tubes and the consuming darkness of underground caverns, hostile feechies and a thousand men bent on his capture. Now his best friend in all the civilized world was climbing steadily toward him to "end this." He suddenly felt overwhelmingly tired. The struggle just didn't seem worth it now, not if he couldn't even count on Steren anymore.

But when Steren was just a few feet away, once he was high enough to be sure no one on the ground could see his face, he gave Aidan a smile and a broad wink. "Run," he whispered through clenched teeth. "And make it look good."

When Aidan leaped from the limb where he stood to a limb on a neighboring tree, Steren was hot after him, careful to jump precisely where he jumped, to land precisely where he landed. For Aidan it was thrilling to be in the forest again with Steren, as they had been so many times when they both lived in Tambluff Castle. For Steren it was no less thrilling. In the years since their famous boar hunt, Steren had often dreamed of that dizzying tree-walk when he followed Dobro and Aidan through the forest canopy to the greenbog. How many times had he wished he hadn't been too tentative and self-conscious to fully enjoy one of the most exhilarating experiences of his life. How many times had he wished for one more chance to soar and leap through the treetops like this. This time he would enjoy it.

Aidan and Steren made the full circuit around Last Camp, in full sight of the Corenwalder soldiers. Viewed from below, their frolic through the treetops looked like a harrowing, death-defying chase. The men were whipped into a frenzy, shouting and whooping like coon hunters following a pack of hounds on the trail. Aidan spiraled upward into the higher boughs, and Steren followed leap for leap, landing for landing, handhold for handhold. Soon they were well out of sight of their audience, up above the overstory.

In the highest branches of an enormous gum tree, the two friends perched like a pair of egrets. Below them they could still hear the clamorous shouts of a thousand men desperate for news of the chase. But here they were above it all. All was peace in the tree-top. Even the whine of mosquitoes, so incessant in the forest as to go largely unnoticed, was absent here. The sun came to them directly, not filtered through the dense leaves of the forest. They had a straight shot to the bluest sky imaginable. Everything seemed clearer here, more focused. Aidan and Steren were boys again, catching their breath after a frolic.

"Remember the last time we did this?" Aidan asked. "With Dobro?" He paused, chuckled. "Things were simpler then."

Steren looked across the river and into feechie country. "I don't know," he said. "Maybe things weren't as simple as we thought they were."

A long silence prevailed. Neither Aidan nor Steren knew quite what to say, where to begin after three years—and such years as those had been. Finally Aidan spoke. "So," he said, in that casual way of people who are just catching up, "how's your father?"

Steren gave Aidan a perplexed look, then got the joke, and he laughed until he almost fell from his perch.

"Father," Steren said when he had regained his composure. "Father . . . he does better than you might think, judging from your run-in this morning. He's rational most of the time—almost all the time, really. But when he's not . . ." Steren's voice trailed off. "I'm the only person left who can talk sense to him when he gets that way. And half the time he won't listen even to me."

"What about the Four and Twenty Noblemen?"

Steren shook his head. "Father doesn't trust any of them anymore. He's outlawed three of them—your father, Aethelbert, and Cleland. Gave their lands to half-wits and flatterers he thought he could control. But now he doesn't trust those men either.

"Think about how many lives are affected every time a king makes a bad decision. Do you ever think about that?"

"No, not really," Aidan admitted.

"I think about it all the time." Steren plucked at the leaves where he sat and watched them flutter down through the overstory when he dropped them. "He's quite sane most of the time," he said. He almost sounded as if he were trying to convince himself. "The best thing I can do is to help manage those times when he's not—try to talk him out of his worst decisions."

"Isn't that strange? Trying to manage a king?"

"Not half so strange as trying to manage your own father."

"What about this invasion of the Feechiefen? You couldn't talk him out of that?"

Steren gave Aidan a wry smile. "Any mention of Aidan Errolson, any whisper about the Wilderking, sends him into an insane rage. There's no talking him out of anything when it comes to you."

"So these Aidanites . . ." Aidan began.

"You know about the Aidanites?"

"Percy told me about them," he said, a little embarrassed.

"Those fools are going to tear this kingdom apart, and they don't seem to care." Aidan saw real anger in the prince's face. "Why they feel the need to force themselves on the ancient prophecies, I'll never know."

"I have nothing to do with those people, you know." Aidan suddenly felt the need to justify himself.

"I know that," Steren answered. "Of course I know that."

"But when you hear about the Aidanites, see what they're doing, does it . . ." Aidan paused. Did he want to know, or did he not want to know? "Does it make you feel bitterness toward me?"

Steren sat quietly, pondering how to answer Aidan's question. "I love Corenwald," he began, slowly. "I don't just mean the throne of Corenwald. I mean Corenwald itself—its people, its lands, its creatures. And if ever I am king, I expect I will go down in history as one of Corenwald's greatest kings. I'm not boasting, I hope you know."

Aidan thought of the admiration that shone so clearly on the faces of the men at Last Camp, and he knew Steren was right. He had grown into a leader of tremendous charisma and ability. He would indeed make a great king.

Steren continued, "And yet I know the Wilderking prophecy. I know it is not God's purpose that the House of Darrow should stand forever.

"But I still haven't answered your question, have I? You asked me whether I ever feel bitterness toward you. Sometimes I do. For the last three years, I've been at Tambluff Castle learning what it is to be a king. And learning the hardest way possible, I don't mind telling you. The burdens I have borne these three years—to watch my father's court disintegrate around him, to be his only comfort and support. Meanwhile, you've been in the Feechiefen Swamp doing who knows what. You had no choice. I understand that. I don't blame you. But I hope you won't blame me either when I say I felt a pang of resentment when I heard people declare that Corenwald never will be happy until Aidan Errolson is its king. Aidan Errolson, who was frolicking with feechies while I was already bearing the burdens of kingship without any of its benefits."

Aidan nodded, humbled by Steren's words. "The Aidanites may be right," Steren continued. "I know they may be right. The time of the Wilderking may be upon us. It may not be the purpose of the living God that I should ever be king." There was evident pain on his face when he spoke. "But I will say this: If *you* are ever to be king"—he pointed a finger at Aidan, not in accusation but for emphasis—"you've got a lot to learn yet—things you can learn only on this side of the river."

Aidan had the strange feeling Steren had outgrown him in the past three years. Steren, who had looked up to Aidan when they were younger, had grown into a man, into someone very like a king. Aidan, on the other hand, felt he was much the same person he had been when he took to the Feechiefen.

At last Aidan spoke. "Steren, I am as loyal to the House of Darrow as I have ever been. And when you inherit the kingdom of Corenwald, God willing, I will be proud to follow you."

"If there is any kingdom left to inherit," Steren said absently, staring across the treetops. Then, with a slight shudder, he came back to the present. "We should be going," he said. "Which way are you headed?"

"West," Aidan answered. "Up the Overland Trail."

"Then I'll go east. I'll circle around and come into Last Camp from the east side, tell the men you escaped that way. That should give you a head start."

Aidan embraced his old friend before they parted ways. "I don't reckon we'll ever talk again like this, will we?"

Steren looked down through the treetops. "No, I don't suppose so. Not so long as my father is king of Corenwald." Looking into his friend's face, he added, "But, Aidan, you'll never have a more devoted friend than I."

WATCH
FOR THE
WILDERKING

Chapter Seven

On the Road
to Hustingreen

obro was showing Percy basic tactics of feechie fighting when Aidan got back to the moss bed where he had left them. Given the head start Steren had provided, they agreed they no longer required the secrecy afforded by treetop travel. They could safely use the Overland Trail, and they would make much better time. Hustingreen was the nearest village. There they could buy supplies, even horses, for the rest of their journey to Sinking Canyons.

They hit the River Road just below Longleaf Manor, Errol's lands, which now belonged to Lord Fershal of the Hill Country. The front fields, once so robust with wheat or sometimes corn, had gone to broomsedge and thistle. Even from the road, they could see that one of the shutters on the front of the manor house was hanging askew.

"Fershal doesn't even live there," Percy remarked. "Spends all his time in Tambluff."

"What about all the farmhands?" Aidan asked. "How do they make a living now?"

Percy shrugged.

"And who's growing food for the villagers in Hustingreen?"

Percy shrugged again. They quickened their pace, eager to put the sad sight of their old home behind them.

The travelers were almost in sight of Hustingreen when they saw the first of the Aidanites' posters. Tacked to a tree on the side of the road, it read in thick, black letters,

WHEN FEAR OF GOD HAS LEFT THE LAND,
TO BE REPLACED BY FEAR OF MAN;
WHEN CORENWALDERS FREE AND TRUE
ENSLAVE THEMSELVES AND OTHERS TOO;

"These foolish people," Aidan grumbled. "They don't know what they're talking about. They don't know what they're doing to Corenwald."

A few steps farther down the road, a second poster was tacked to a tree on the other side:

WHEN JUSTICE AND MERCY DISAPPEAR,
WHEN LIFE IS CHEAP AND GOLD IS DEAR,

Aidan snatched the sheet of palmetto paper from the tree and ripped it in half, then half and half again. "How I'd like to rip the man who put these up," he growled.

Dobro watched Aidan carefully, not sure what to make of his behavior. He couldn't read and wouldn't have recognized the Wilderking Chant even if he could read. He assumed this was a strange civilizer custom.

Aidan snatched the next poster:

TO THE PALACE HE COMES FROM FORESTS AND SWAMPS.
WATCH FOR THE WILDERKING!

And the next:

LEADING HIS TROOPS OF WILD MEN AND BRUTES.
WATCH FOR THE WILDERKING!

Aidan was furious. These meddlers, these Aidanites, couldn't leave well enough alone, could they? They had to stir up trouble, had to force themselves on the ancient prophecies. Now Aidan's family was outlawed and living in the most godforsaken patch of ground in all of Corenwald; the civilizers had narrowly missed all-out war with the feechies; Aidan was running for his life and would never see his beloved Feechiefen again—all because of his so-called followers and their posters.

HE WILL SILENCE THE BRAGGART,
ENNOBLE THE COWARD.
WATCH FOR THE WILDERKING!

Aidan snatched it down and stomped on it. "I'd like to silence a braggart or two," he observed.

JUSTICE WILL ROLL, AND MERCY WILL TOLL.
WATCH FOR THE WILDERKING!

"Let me do this one," Dobro suggested. He was eager to adopt the ways of the civilizers, however strange they seemed. He contorted his face into a fierce scowl, imitating Aidan's expression. He ripped the paper from the tree, balled it up, and jumped up and down on it, bringing his knees almost up to his chin with each jump and flailing his arms. "I'll bragger the silence," he snarled. "I'll fool the folks what don't know what they're doing." Percy doubled over laughing at Dobro's bad imitation of Aidan's outbursts. "Looks like the Aidanites have a new enemy," he said. Aidan couldn't help smiling himself, in spite of his irritation.

Dobro was still jumping up and down on the Aidanites' poster when three men emerged from the forest. They were older than the three travelers, well into their forties. Each wore a tunic of green homespun and a flattened black hat adorned with an egret feather. All three wore swords, though the swords looked like something they might have found in a grandfather's old trunk. They looked familiar to Aidan; they were villagers he had seen at the Hustingreen market growing up, but he had never known their names. A red-bearded fellow appeared to be the leader of the trio.

When he swaggered up to Dobro, the feechie stopped what he was doing and looked curiously at the red beard thrust within a foot of his face.

The villager looked Dobro up and down, from his matted hair (it hadn't come clean during his bath in the Tam) to his one black eyebrow, to his gap-toothed mouth, receding chin, and prominent Adam's apple to his thin, hard arms and legs and bare feet, and finally to the crumpled wad of palmetto paper beneath them. He had never seen anyone like this scrawny, pinch-faced lunatic defacing the poster he had hand lettered himself. "Just what do you think you're doing?" he asked.

Dobro looked down at his feet, a little surprised that the fellow had to ask. "I think I'm stompin' on a piece of paper I snatched offa that there tree," he answered, pointing a black-nailed finger toward the tree he spoke of. "Now that I think about it," he clarified, "I *know* that's what I'm doin'. And when I find the fool what tacked it to the tree, I'm gonna tear him into little pieces."

"Well, you're in luck, stranger," said the red-bearded man. "'Cause you just found the man who put that poster up."

"Haa-wee!" Dobro shouted, clapping joyfully. "That was a heap easier than I figured on!" He felt sure he would fit in fine among the civilizers if they were all like this red-bearded fellow. He hopped a circle around the Hustingreener with his fists raised. "Come on, civilizer," he called, "let's mix it!"

Dobro's opponent looked at him with astonishment. "Who *are* you?" he asked. Dobro stopped hopping. Of course! A feechie fight had to start off with a rudeswap. A civilizer fight, apparently, had to start off with introductions. He was still learning civilizer ways. "I'm Dobro Turtlebane," he said, "from Bug Neck." He jerked a thumb over his shoulder, pointing southwest toward the swamp he called home.

"Bug Neck?" said the red-bearded man. "Never heard of it."

"You know, Bug Neck," Dobro repeated. "A day's polin' east of Scoggin Mound?" The villager still looked blank. Dobro was a little annoyed. "In the Feechiefen!"

The three Hustingreeners squinted at Dobro. "Feechiefen?" one of them muttered. Then it dawned on them. No wonder this fellow looked so strange and acted even stranger. "He's a feechie!" one of the men gasped.

The three men stared wide-eyed at one another. The sandy-haired one was the first to speak. He quoted a snatch of the Wilderking Chant: "'Leading his troops of wild men and brutes.'" And together the three of them quoted the next line in reverent tones: "'Watch for the Wilderking!'"

"This is a sign," the red-bearded man said to his companions. "This fellow's a sign, I'm telling you. If there's a feechie in Hustingreen, Aidan Errolson can't be far behind."

"You said something there, feller," Dobro said.

"Matter of fact, he ain't no more'n five or six steps behind."

The Hustingreeners looked past Dobro to Percy and Aidan. They had found Dobro so peculiar that they had paid very little attention to the civilizers with him. Aidan's looks had changed since he had last gone to market in Hustingreen, but now that they had a good look at him, the three villagers recognized him.

"Aidan Errolson," one of them said in hushed tones.

"Hail to the Wilderking," said another. His eyes were glistening with tears of joy.

The three Hustingreeners elbowed past each other to be the first to kneel at Aidan's feet.

"Your Majesty!"

"Our king in exile, returned to us!"

"Command us, our sovereign!"

Their voices quivered with emotion.

"Get up! Get up!" Aidan demanded. There was anger in his voice. Embarrassed, he looked around to be sure no one else had seen this unseemly display. "Your king is Darrow, not me," he said sharply as he waded through the kneeling Aidanites.

"Listen to him," said one of the Aidanites as they scrambled to their feet to follow him. "He's so humble."

"Nothing like King Darrow. Not like King Darrow at all."

"That's what Corenwald needs in a king—somebody who's not going to try to grab all the power for himself."

Aidan stalked with long strides toward the village, and Percy and Dobro strode with him. The three Aidanites trotted to keep up.

"I'm Milum," said the red-bearded fellow, "and this is Burson and Wash." Aidan didn't even acknowledge them and didn't offer to introduce his brother Percy who, though he understood this was a serious situation, was finding it very hard not to laugh at the absurdity of it all.

"We just knew you'd come straight to Hustingreen when you came back." Milum had begun speaking so fast he could hardly catch his breath. "I remember when you were a boy. You probably don't remember me, but I remember you. You'd come on market days, and one day you kicked a ball under my cart and I kicked it back. But you probably don't remember." He paused a moment to give Aidan a chance to say something like "Sure, of course I remember that," but Aidan looked straight ahead as if he hadn't heard anything. *So this is what Aidanites look like,* he thought. *So these are the fools threatening to tear this kingdom apart.*

They were within a hundred strides of the village of Hustingreen by now. Burson and Wash ran ahead shouting, "Aidan Errolson is here!" and "The Wilderking is returned!"

Meanwhile Milum continued his monologue. "Hustingreen's a major Aidanite stronghold, you know. Of course you know. It's almost your home village. Everybody in Hustingreen has an Aidan Errolson story. Every old lady in the village says she could tell, even when you were a little boy, you would grow up to do great things."

Percy pinched Aidan's cheek, a gesture that had always made him redden when he was a little boy. He slapped Percy's hand away.

Milum yammered on. "Just yesterday an old boy at the militia drills was telling a story about the time you . . ."

Aidan stopped in his tracks. "Militia drills?" He looked hard at Milum. "What militia?"

Milum laughed a nervous laugh, not sure whether Aidan was putting him on. "Why, the Aidanite Militia, Hustingreen unit." He stood up straight, raised his chin, and popped his right fist against his heart. This, apparently, was the Aidanite salute. He gestured to his green tunic and plumed hat. "This is the Aidanite uniform."

Aidan could feel his face grow hot. "This militia," he said, barely able to keep his voice down. "Whom do you propose to fight?"

Milum looked askance at Aidan. Surely Aidan was pulling his leg now. "Of course you know *that!*" he began. But seeing Aidan's eyes narrow, he cleared his throat, straightened his posture, and recited the official answer: "The purpose of the Aidanite Militia is to stand in readiness to protect the motherland from all who would threaten the common good . . . sir!" He gave Aidan a knowing wink.

The impertinence on Milum's face infuriated Aidan. "Don't you know that this is treason?" he shouted.

"To train yourselves to fight against your king? If you think I would lead a revolt against King Darrow—my king, your king—you are mightily mistaken!"

Milum's shoulders slumped and his head dropped. He was crushed by Aidan's strong words. But Aidan didn't care. He was furious. A traitor deserved much more than harsh words.

But neither Milum nor Aidan had long to reflect on the exchange. From Hustingreen they heard the peal of bells in the village square, and it looked as if the whole village was running out to meet them on the road.

Percy, Dobro, and Aidan considered running away, but the happy throng was on them before they could make a decisive move. People were shouting, dogs barking and children laughing. A pair of buglers played a tinny and off-key version of a local folk tune. A kind-faced old woman handed Aidan a pie that had been cooling in her window when the news came that the Wilderking was come at last. The village girls all kissed Percy and Aidan. A few of the brave ones even kissed Dobro.

In a confused moment, a group of men tried to hoist Percy onto their shoulders, mistaking him for Aidan. Wash straightened them out, and they scooped up Aidan in spite of his protests. Others lifted Percy and Dobro to their shoulders for good measure, and the whole procession marched back into Hustingreen, led by the red-faced, white-bearded village mayor, who swung his staff of office like a parade marshal's baton.

Chapter Eight

The Aidanites' Rally

he mob was so raucous, so joyous, the people didn't seem to notice Aidan's protests. There was such jostling and bumping the men carrying Aidan didn't even pay any mind to his wiggling efforts to get off their shoulders. Percy steered his bearers toward his brother, and when he was next to Aidan's ear, he shouted, "Stop struggling! Let's just go with it! You'll get your chance to make a speech. Then you can set everybody straight!" He nearly fell off when one of the men carrying him tripped over a dog. "But shouldn't we find out as much about these Aidanites as we can?"

Aidan nodded. For the moment at least, he had no choice but to "go with it." And Percy was right: The more he knew about his "followers," the better he could undo the damage they had done. But he also had the nagging suspicion that his brother's suggestion was motivated not by prudence but by his appetite for the ridiculous.

Dobro, for his part, was having tremendous fun. To a feechie, a roiling mob looked a lot like a regular party. The scene was downright homey for Dobro, unaware as he was of the larger trouble it represented. He took every hand that reached up to him. He waved at the children, many of whom ran away in terror. Dobro was almost as big an attraction as Aidan himself, being the only feechie the Hustingreeners had ever seen.

The buglers were joined along the way by a drummer and a xylophone player. It wasn't clear, however, whether they were trying to play the same tune. The mayor, in his self-important way, led the procession to the middle of the village square, where trading was done on market days. A general murmur quickly grew into a loud, rhythmic chant: "Speech! Speech! Speech!"

Aidan was more than happy to make a speech. It was going to be a stem-winder too. He was going to set these people good and straight. But before he could collect his thoughts, the mayor bounded to the platform in the middle of the square (he was surprisingly agile for a man of such roundness) and raised his hands for silence.

"For years we have labored in the dark shadow of tyranny," he began in deep, dramatic tones.

"Tell it, Mayor!" came a woman's voice from the crowd.

"No more tyrants!" A man in a wool cap shook his fist in the air.

The mayor raised his hands again in acknowledgment of his hearers' comments and kept going. "Too long have the wrongs of an unjust ruler been heaped on the backs of hardworking villagers like yourselves."

"My back's killing me!" called a voice in the crowd.

"Hear him!"

"Yes-s-s-s!"

"Where are the young men of Hustingreen?" asked the mayor. Moans from the audience. "I ask you, where are our young men?" Young wives throughout the crowd began to cry loudly. Aidan noticed for the first time that, except for Percy, Dobro, and himself, the crowd was composed entirely of children, women, and men over forty.

"*Drafted into Darrow's army,* that's where!" The mayor shook with indignation as he answered his own question. "Dragged off to the Feechiefen Swamp to fight for a king who doesn't care if he throws away the lives of his own subjects!"

The wailing of women grew louder. The mayor paused for silence. Or was he just enjoying the effect of his own oratory? "But today a new light has dawned!" An approving murmur rippled through the square. "The Wilderking prophecy has been the only hope of an unhappy people. Today it is coming true!" The murmur grew louder. "Today Aidan Errolson has come out of the swamps and forests—just as the Wilderking prophecy said he would—back to his people, who have longed for his return!" The mayor had to shout to be heard over the rapturous crowd. "Hail to the Wilderking!"

"Hail to the Wilderking!" the people replied in a deafening shout.

Aidan's face was ghostly white. This was much worse than he had imagined it would be. He felt as if he might faint.

A group of schoolchildren was herded onto the platform. A polite silence fell over the crowd as the spectators turned their attention toward the children who, as their tutor proudly explained, had memorized the Wilderking Chant in class.

The recitation got off to a ragged start. One of the boys obviously didn't have it down yet; he appeared to be mouthing the words "Watermelon, watermelon, watermelon," and his hand motions were a full second behind those of his peers. But the rest of the children's confidence grew, and by the time they had reached "Watch for the Wilderking," the crowd joined in on the refrain in a kind of responsive reading.

It would have been quite a moving experience, this public recitation from the old lore, if Aidan didn't understand what it all meant. When the children reached the line "Watch for the Wilderking, widows and orphans," a widow in the fifth row raised her hands and fainted rapturously away.

When the children had shuffled off the stage, a mime troupe reenacted the Battle of Bonifay Plain. The players had to cut it short, however, when the mime playing Greidawl the giant fell off his stilts and wrenched his knee. It was all so ridiculous, Percy couldn't help howling with laughter.

Eighteen years old, Aidan thought, *and I've already passed into legend.* The villagers, in fact, were so taken with the legendary version of Aidan being presented on the stage that they paid surprisingly little attention to the real Aidan. They gave a very warm welcome to the bard who stood to sing "The Ballad of Aidan Errolson." All of Hustingreen seemed quite familiar with this versified (though not precisely accurate) account of his first expedition into the Feechiefen:

It's a dangerous thing to be feared by a king,
And Aidan struck dread in King Darrow.
His most loyal service just made the king nervous
And pierced his black heart like an arrow.

One feast night the king sentenced Aidan to death
As he sat in his pride and his pomp.
He said with tongue forkéd, "I want a frog orchid,
And it grows in the Feechiefen Swamp, boy,
Nowhere but the Feechiefen Swamp."

Oh weep, won't you weep for a kingdom whose
  royalty
Can't tell high treason from untainted loyalty.

It seems funny, don't it, that the old boy who
  wanted
The orchid sat safe in his hall
While the bold son of Errol ran headlong toward
  peril
And dispraised his king not at all.

Young Aidan was neither the first nor the only
To outdare the vast Feechiefen.
There were brave men of yore who dared to
  explore,
But none of them came out again, boys.
Nobody comes back again.

I ask you, what good kings—who else but
  dictators—
Send subjects to get et by panthers and gators?

Last Camp hangs grim at the kingdom's far limit.
Beyond it? That's anyone's guess.
Beyond it, pure mystery throughout all of history.
But beyond it lay young Aidan's quest.

At the great river's bend lives a tough breed of
  men;
The Last Campers fear very few.
But they said with a shiver, "If you cross that
  river,
Dear Aidan, we sure will miss you, boy,
Dear Aidan, we sure will miss you."

Aidan stood by the Tam with his pack in his hand
And watched where the brown water swirled.
He said his good-byes to all things civilized,
Then he stepped off the edge of the world, boys.
He stepped off the edge of the world.

Could you face the Feechiefen, there take your
    chances?
Could you leave your country with no backward
    glances?

Aidan went for to wander way over yonder
Where graybeard moss sways in the breeze.
Where gator jaws snap and craney-crows flap
And moccasins drop from the trees.

Who knows what occurred? No one ever heard.
Our young hero never did say.
But he somehow survived where so many men died
And he brung the frog orchid away, boys.
He brung the frog orchid away.

And thereby was proven, or so it would seem,
Young Errolson's friendship and love for the king.

Back at the palace, King Darrow the jealous
Mused on the murder he'd planned.
Imagine his gloom when the boy he had doomed
Marched in with the orchid in hand.

Aidan soon understood that his gift was no good,
So he wheeled and ran swiftly away.
He returned again to the deep Feechiefen,
And there he has stayed to this day, boys.
There he has stayed to this day.

The crowd was delighted, but Aidan had heard enough. He pushed his way to the front and mounted the platform. The crowd roared at the sight of him, and the chant quickly arose again: "Hail to the Wilderking! Hail to the Wilderking!"

"Quiet!" Aidan shouted over the noise. "Be quiet! Let me speak!"

Gradually the noise subsided enough for Aidan to make himself heard. "People of Hustingreen!" he yelled. "You have a king! His name is Darrow!"

Hissing sounded from the audience. "Darrow ain't my king!" a voice called.

"Hail to the Wilderking! Hail to the Wilderking!"

"No!" Aidan shouted. "No! This is treason! This is a gathering of traitors!"

Percy watched with some concern as smiling faces turned sullen and grumbling rumbled across the village square.

But Aidan didn't care. "I will have no part of this." He remembered something Bayard the Truthspeaker had told him years before, and he repeated it to the Hustingreeners. "A traitor is no fit king. How can a man be king of Corenwald if he betrays the king of Corenwald?"

Quizzical looks contorted a few faces as Aidan's hearers tried to work out the tricky logic of the question.

"Looks to me like Darrow's the traitor," the village blacksmith shouted. "The way I figure, he's the one who ain't fit to be king!" Heads began nodding again. People were slapping the blacksmith's back and shaking his hand.

Aidan could tell he was losing them again. "People of Hustingreen! Aidanites!" he yelled, straining to be heard. "It is not your job to make the ancient prophecies come true!"

"We ain't making the prophecies come true," Wash yelled back. "You're doing a fine job of that your own self!" The crowd laughed and whooped in appreciation. Wash pressed his advantage. "Aidan Errolson, did you or did you not kill a panther with a stone?"

"Well, yes," Aidan admitted. "But . . ."

"He did, he did!" Dobro yodeled. "I seen it with these two eyes!" Dobro had gotten caught up in the mob's enthusiasm. But a stern look from Aidan silenced him.

"'With a stone he shall quell the panther fell!'" Wash triumphantly quoted the Wilderking Chant, sticking his chest out and jabbing a finger in Aidan's direction.

"'He will silence the braggart, ennoble the coward,'" piped an old veteran, also quoting from the chant. "I was there at Bonifay, young man. I saw that braggart giant go silent. I was one of the warriors of Corenwald who were ennobled again in our most fearful hour."

"Where you been these three years, Aidan Errolson?" asked a woman Aidan recognized as the village baker.

"Feechiefen," Aidan mumbled.

"I'm sorry," the woman called sweetly. "I didn't hear that last part."

Aidan cleared his throat and spoke more loudly. "The Feechiefen Swamp."

"Interesting," the woman said. Then she lowered her voice for dramatic effect and recited the last three lines of the Wilderking Chant:

Look to the swamplands, ye misfit, ye outcast.
From the land's wildest places a wild man will
come
To give the land back to his people.

"I'm ready to get my land back!" bellowed somebody in the back.

"Me too!" yelled another. "When do we get started?"

The village square erupted again with raucous laughter and good-natured jostling.

"Hear me!" Aidan screamed as loudly as he could. "Hear this well! I will have nothing to do with any rebellion against the king! I will not stand by, either, and let anyone revolt in my name!" But nobody heard him or paid him any mind.

Aidan jumped off the platform to rejoin Percy and Dobro. "Let's get out of here!" he still had to shout to be heard, even though he was standing beside them. "These people are all fools or traitors!"

"That may be!" Percy shouted back. "But that doesn't mean they've got it all wrong!"

Chapter Nine

The Boss of the Forest

idan, Dobro, and Percy gave up on getting supplies for their journey to Sinking Canyons. Now all they wanted was to get away from Hustingreen; but that proved to be no easy matter. A group of boys noticed them trying to slip out of the village and followed them, whooping, capering, and pushing each other. Soon the whole village was following them north on the River Road, as if they were on a pleasure outing.

"To Tambluff!" somebody yelled. They were, after all, headed in the direction of the capital city.

"Hurray!" the crowd shouted in response.

Aidan could hear the boisterous, happy conversation between several old men near the front of the crowd. "You gotta like his style," said one of them. "Bold, determined."

"I'm with you," said another. "We know the king ain't there; he's off at the swamp with our boys."

"Hee-hee," laughed the first. "King Darrow's in for a surprise when he gets home, ain't he?"

"But don't you reckon he left somebody guarding the castle?" suggested a third man.

But the other two seemed unconcerned. "Don't you worry about that, old boy. If I know Aidan Errolson, he's got a plan."

Aidan Errolson did have a plan, but it had nothing to do with storming Tambluff Castle. Taking the River Road was only a ruse. The last thing they needed was a whole village of Aidanites following them to their hideout in Sinking Canyons. Their true destination lay many leagues to the west and south, far from the River Road—far indeed from any road.

On Dobro's signal, the three disappeared into the forest on the left side of the road, clambering up a convenient tree and soaring through the treetops, hidden from the wondering eyes of the Hustingreeners.

Dobro led the way to the banks of Bayberry Creek. They waded the creek, pausing to cool themselves and to drink of the black water before pushing on to the west and south.

The tangled forest of the bottomlands opened up into a great pine savannah a few leagues below the Bayberry. Confident that the Aidanites couldn't possibly have tracked them, the three travelers returned to the ground and continued their trek on foot, careful to avoid the few small farms, turpentine camps, and other tiny settlements that dotted the landscape in this part of the island.

By midmorning on the second day after they had left Hustingreen, even those small, isolated settlements were nowhere to be found. Aidan, Dobro, and Percy were entering Corenwald's Clay Wastes. Unlike most of the island, here the soil was too poor for farming. Even the forests looked thin and degraded. The stately old longleaf pines of the upland savannah were replaced by scrubby second-growth pine trees. A few trees were as tall as seventy or eighty feet, but even those were so spindly they looked as if a good strong wind might snap them in two. In some places the trees formed dense thickets. In others, they were so far apart that even a person with a strong arm could hardly throw a rock from one tree to the next. Without the protection of the longleaf overstory, the waving wiregrass was overrun by vines and briars. It was exactly the kind of vegetation that made tree walking necessary, but the trees were too irregularly spaced for that.

"You won't be finding no feechies in this part of the island," Dobro grunted as he slashed through a briar bush with a pole he had cut from a turkey oak. "Can't swim, can't boat, can't tree-walk."

"So we're going to be living in a place that's too wild for the feechiefolk," Aidan mumbled.

Dobro slapped at the back of his neck and danced with rage. His skin, so white after his first bath, was now an angry red from sunburn and splotched with the purple welts raised by mosquitoes and other biting insects that swarmed in all of Corenwald's wild places.

"These bugs is about to chaw me down to bones and tallow," Dobro complained. "How can you civilizers go pirootin' around without no mud cover and not go crazy account of the itching?"

"We're just tougher than feechies, I suppose," Percy said, cutting his eyes over toward Dobro to see his reaction.

Dobro slapped at another bug. "If I wasn't so miserable," he said, "I'd whup both of you and show you how tough a feechie is." He gave a little wiggle, rubbing his knees together to scratch matching mosquito bites on the inside of either knee.

Dobro moaned, "I don't mind telling you, these skeeters done whupped and defeated me."

"Dobro, you ought to be ashamed of yourself," Percy chided. "A full-grown feechie defeated by mosquitoes."

"There ain't no shame in that," said Dobro. "No shame at all. You know who's the boss of the forest, don't you?"

"I don't know," said Percy. "A bear? A panther? Certainly not a mosquito."

Dobro gave another slap at his bare arm and launched into a story meant to educate his fellow travelers and keep his own mind off his troubles.

"Mr. Wildcat and Mr. Alligator got to argufying about who was the boss of the forest. Up and down they had it, back and forth, who should and who shouldn't. They got so aggravated till Mr. Wildcat finally reached back with his off-paw and fetched one across Mr. Alligator's snout. *Ker-blip!* "

Dobro reenacted the blow, swinging his open hand in a sweeping, roundhouse motion.

"Well now, Mr. Alligator was astonished that his old friend Mr. Wildcat would strike a blow against him. His eyes filled up with tears. He turned tail like he was headed back into the water, and Mr. Wildcat figured he'd made his point. He sat down on his hunkers and mewed out a song:

None of you critters better give me sauce.
I am the champeen, I am the boss.
Boss of this river, boss of these trees.
All of you critters better ask me please.

"But Mr. Alligator's tearfulness was just a trick he learnt from Cousin Crocodile. He didn't even feel that cat's furry paw against his bony snout. And he sure didn't have it in his mind to skedaddle from such a fight as that. Naw, he turnt tail so he could reach that sassy wildcat better.

"Mr. Wildcat was strokin' his chin whiskers and feelin' mighty bumptious when Mr. Alligator's tail come whippin' 'round like a harrycane. That poor cat was flung nearbout to the other side of the river. And by the time he'd paddled to the far bank, lookin' droopy and bedraggled, Mr. Wildcat decided not to pursue the question no further with Mr. Alligator.

"Wasn't too much longer before Mr. Bear come by and seen Mr. Alligator looking biggety. He asked him, 'What makes you hold your head so high, Mr. Alligator?'

"Alligator given him one of them long smiles of his, and then he sings out,

None of you critters better give me sauce.
I am the champeen, I am the boss.
Boss of this river, boss of these trees.
All of you critters better ask me please.

"Mr. Bear figured on that a while, and then he suggested maybe Mr. Alligator weren't the boss after all, and they commenced to argufyin'. Up and down they had it, back and forth, who can and who can't, who is and who isn't. They got so aggravated that Mr. Alligator reached way back with his tail and frammed Mr. Bear across the hunkers.

"That hurted Mr. Bear, you know. But mostly it made him mad. Mr. Bear's a big feller and don't fling so easy as a wildcat. He reached up high with his near paw and *kerflunked* it right down betwixt Mr. Alligator's knobbly eyes just like he was swingin' a hammer. Knocked all the bubbles out'n him. Sunk him all the way to the river mud. Mr. Alligator figured he'd had about all he wanted, and he moseyed a good piece down the river afore he knobbed his nose out'n the water again.

"Mr. Bear couldn't help bloviatin' a little bit.

He stood up on his behind legs and grumbled and growled so as to get his pitch, then he sung out:

None of you critters better give me sauce.
I am the champeen, I am the boss.
Boss of this river, boss of these trees.
All of you critters better ask me please.

"Then Mr. Bear figured that if he was going to be the boss of the forest he better go ahead and start bossin' some folks. So he gathered up all the critters in a clearing where he could give everybody their 'signments. The critters didn't like it very much, and they all was grumblin' in their goozlums, but they'd seen what Mr. Bear done to Mr. Alligator, and them what didn't see it had heard about it. Nobody figured he'd be the first person to backchat Mr. Bear.

"Mr. Bear said, 'You folks probably heard already, I'm the boss of this here forest.' That made the critters feel uneasy in their minds, but nobody said nothin'. They just kind of shuffled their paws around a little bit.

"Then, when Mr. Bear was about to start with the 'signments, somebody hollered out, 'I don't reckon you the boss of me, old Bear.'

"Mr. Bear's brow went wrinkly and he stared from critter to critter. He asked, 'Which one of you folks is givin' me sauce?' All the critters just looked down at their paws, afraid Mr. Bear would think it was them what said he weren't the boss. Mr. Bear said a little louder, 'Which one of you critters is givin' me sauce?'

"The voice hollered out again, 'I'm the one what's givin' you sauce, Bear. That's the way I like my bear meat—with a little sauce.'

"Mr. Bear ain't grumblin' no more. Now he's roaring: 'Who said that?!'

"The voice hollered out a third time: 'It's me, it's Mr. Flea. And I don't mind saying, I'm a better man than you, Mr. Bear.'

"Mr. Bear squinched up his eyes and soodled down close to the ground and sure enough, he seen Mr. Flea standing on the top of a daisy flower with his chest poked out and his fists balled up. Mr. Bear give a snort, then he commenced to hee-hawing.

"That just made Mr. Flea mad. 'I ain't a man to be laughed at,' he told him. 'You better 'pologize to me, and in a hurry too.'

"But Mr. Bear'd done flopped down on the ground and was tee-heein' and haw-hawin' like he just couldn't help hisself.

"Mr. Flea poked out his chest farther and balled up his fists harder. 'You stand up and show me some respect, Bear, or you gonna find out why!'

"But it weren't no use. Mr. Bear guffawed and rolled around like somebody was ticklin' him in the short ribs. Well, Mr. Flea weren't one to make idle threats. He was a man of action. He hopped off that daisy flower and onto Mr. Bear's nose. Found a nice soft spot and got hisself a whole mouthful.

"You can believe Mr. Bear stopped laughing then. He raised up a paw and swatted his snout so hard that he knocked his own slobber all over Mr. Possum. But Mr. Flea was long gone. He hopped up to Mr. Bear's ear and got hisself another plug of bear hide. Mr. Bear 'bout knocked hisself cross-eyed punchin' at his own ear, but by that time Mr. Flea had done attached himself to Mr. Bear's hindquarters.

"Mr. Bear flopped on his back and wallowed around, but Mr. Flea already commenced to chawin' on his belly. Then he got him up under the chin, then up under his left armpit."

Dobro paused for dramatic effect. "And do you know what that bear done then?" Percy and Aidan shook their heads, eager to hear the end of the story.

"He sat there and took it, that's what he did. What else could he do? Mr. Flea was gnawin' the hide off'n him, and he couldn't do one thing to stop him.

"Finally Mr. Flea spit out a mouthful of bristle and gristle and hollered out, 'How 'bout it, Mr. Bear? You surrender?' And you can believe the critters perked up to hear the answer to that question.

"Mr. Bear moaned, all humble-come-tumble, 'I surrender, Mr. Flea! Mercy!'

"Mr. Flea stood on Mr. Bear's nose and looked him in the eye. He said, 'I ain't a hard man, Mr. Bear, but I ain't gonna let nobody boss me or my people. You hear me, Bear?'

"'I hear you, Mr. Flea.'

"And the flea sung a different song:

I like my bear with a little sauce.
This here forest got a brand-new boss!

"And so," Dobro concluded, "if a flea can be a better man than a bear, I ain't going to feel so bad about getting whupped by a whole swarm of mosquitoes."

Dobro looked up and down his exposed arms and legs. He still couldn't get used to them being any color but the gray of swamp mud. "I was plenty pink after you tried to scrub my skin off at the river," he said. "But I keep gettin' pinker by the minute. Next seep hole or stagnant pool we come to, I aim to wallow in it."

"No, you won't!" Aidan and Percy said in unison.

"If you want to live among civilizers, you've got to live *like* civilizers," Aidan said. "You aren't subjecting my family to that feechie stink. Your breath alone is going to be as much as most civilizers can stand."

"Besides," Percy added, "we're almost to Sinking Canyons already. Next water we see will be the little creek that flows at the bottom of the canyons."

Chapter Ten

Into the Canyons

The morning of the third day after leaving Hustingreen, the three travelers struck a little creek that was struggling across the plain. "This is it," said Percy. "This is the creek that flows through Sinking Canyons."

Aidan took another look at the muddy stream. He could easily jump across it. It wasn't even deep enough to support fish larger than minnows and shiners. He cocked his head and looked questioningly at Percy. "This little creek cut a canyon?" Aidan had seen a canyon once in the Hill Country. Through it roared the Upper Branch of the mighty River Tam, boiling white as it leaped over rocks and plunged into pools, swirling and thundering, cutting its own path through the canyon's granite walls on its way to the sea many leagues away. Aidan could imagine the River Tam cutting a canyon. But this little stream? It didn't seem possible.

As they hiked up the stream, however, its banks deepened and grew farther apart. And soon the banks of the creek weren't banks anymore, but the sides of a little valley through which the stream ran flat and wide, not even ankle deep, in muddy rivulets that crossed and recrossed one another like braided hair.

"Watch this," said Percy as he stepped into the braided stream. The water ran over the tops of his feet and flowed cloudier a little distance before the stirred-up mud settled out again. Percy pointed where he had just stepped. "Watch my bootprints." The clear imprint of Percy's boots melted away as the rivulets braided themselves back together in the soft mud. "A hundred men could troop up this streambed, and a quarter hour later there would be no trace of them." The stream was forever shifting, constantly flowing into new patterns of its own design. There, out in the open, was a secret passageway of sorts, covering tracks almost as quickly as the travelers could make them.

Before long the streambed had sunk more deeply beneath the level of the plain. The steep sides of the valley were noticeably higher than the three travelers' heads, and Dobro was growing visibly nervous. "This ain't no place for a feechie," he said. "I got no business going underneath the ground."

"You aren't underground," Aidan said, pointing at the mud they were slogging through. "There's the ground, and it's under you."

"That ain't the ground I'm talkin' 'bout," Dobro answered. He pointed up the valley wall to the grass and trees that grew well above them. "I'm talkin' 'bout that ground." He began moaning the warning chant that his mother had taught him about Sinking Canyons:

Fallen are the feechiefolks,
In a gully, down a hole.
No more fistfights, no more jokes,
In a gully, down a hole.
To the river, to the woods,
In a gully, down a hole.
Time to leave these neighborhoods.
In a gully, down a hole.

By now the valley had deepened into a canyon. Its sheer walls were so high that not even Dobro could heave a rock up to the canyon rim. Aidan had never seen another place like it. The midday sun reflecting off the sheer canyon walls was almost blinding. Up near the rim, at the top of the canyon wall ran a band of the same red clay that prevailed throughout much of Corenwald. But below that, and all the way down to the canyon floor, the wall was a swirl of colors ranging from white to deep pink to lavender and every combination thereof.

The farther they traveled up the canyon, the higher the walls rose above them, to fifty feet, to a hundred feet, even to a hundred fifty feet in places. On either side the walls folded themselves into fissures and crevices. In places they bulged out in rounded buttresses like the base of a swamp tree. On either hand numerous fingers, smaller canyons, connected to the main canyon like tributaries joining a river. They created a mazelike complex of caves and hidey-holes—a perfect place for lying low, an easy place to defend against a much larger force, if need be. Knife-thin ridges, some a hundred feet high, spurred out from the canyon walls. The canyon floor was dotted with great pink and white chimneys and towers, some round and boulderlike, some so high and spindly they looked as if they might topple over any minute.

"Time to leave these neighborhoods," Dobro repeated, remembering his mother's warnings.

But Aidan was fascinated with the place. "What is it made of?" he asked, admiring the breathtaking beauty of the scene. "Some sort of stone?"

"Not stone," Percy answered, leading his brother to the nearest spur. He swiped his hand across the surface of the wall, and a shower of sand cascaded to the ground. Then he held his hand up to Aidan's face, showing him the layer of slick white clay that remained. "Sand and clay," he said, waving his hand to gesture around him. "This whole canyon is nothing but clay and tight-packed sand."

A hundred strides up the canyon, Percy pointed up at a tree that dangled upside down against the canyon wall, half its roots still clinging to the red soil at the canyon's rim. "That tree was still standing when we got here two years ago," Percy said. "Fell in when the ground beneath it collapsed in a rainstorm last year." He pointed at a second tree nearby whose roots snaked out of the clay and into midair. "That one is liable to go next."

Dobro swung a few steps toward the far side of the canyon, as if he expected the tree to crash down on him any second. "Time to leave these neighborhoods," he muttered, but neither Errolson paid him any mind. "Trees falling down," Dobro continued under his breath, "sand walls liable to drop off and bury us alive . . ."

"All right, Dobro," Aidan said, "we know: Sinking Canyons is no place for a feechie."

"That's what I been trying to tell you!" Dobro answered. "No vines to swing on. Nothing but scrubbified trees that ain't hardly worth climbing. Ain't even enough water to get the hairy part of my foot wet—" He suddenly broke off. "What was that?" he whispered, pointing at a low chimney nearby. "'Hind of that big rock." He picked up a hardened lump of white clay about the size of his fist, and when the top of a head appeared from behind the chimney, he cut loose with the clay ball, which whistled mere inches from sandy curls that quickly disappeared again behind the chimney.

"A spy!" Dobro yelled. "I ain't gonna tolerate a feller spyin' on me like he was a bunny in a brush pile. It ain't neighborly." He had already picked up another jagged clay ball when Percy grabbed his throwing arm.

"Hold on, fireball," Percy laughed. "It's one of our sentries." He cupped his hands around his mouth and shouted toward the chimney. "Slider Turtle!" That was the password.

A hand waved from behind the chimney. "You can come out," Percy called. "All is clear."

"Arliss!" Percy shouted when the sentry came out.

"Arliss?" Aidan called after him, delighted to see the young miner who once led him through the caverns under the Bonifay Plain six years earlier.

Arliss rubbed his eyes. "Aidan, is that you?"

"It's me," Aidan answered, and the two young men stood looking at one another, not sure what to say. "You still don't look much like a miner," Aidan finally said, looking up and down his old friend's long and lanky frame.

"But I still got the miner's head," Arliss said, tapping his skull with a skinny finger. "And that's worth plenty with the boys at Greasy Cave."

"This is Dobro," Aidan said by way of introduction. "Dobro, this is Arliss."

Arliss extended a hand to shake with Dobro, but Dobro didn't seem to notice as he flashed a greenish, gappy grin at the civilizer and stepped up to give him a head-butt of greeting and good fellowship, in the feechie manner.

Aidan grabbed Dobro's arm to stop him, lest he should break the taller man's nose with his forehead. He discreetly gestured at Arliss's outstretched hand. After a moment of confusion, Dobro placed his clay ball in Arliss's hand—the same clay ball he had meant to throw at Arliss's head a few moments earlier.

"Dobro's a . . ." Aidan wasn't sure he was ready to go into the details. "Dobro's an old friend."

Arliss kept smiling, but his eyes narrowed the least bit, as if he were trying to figure this strange fellow out.

"From the Feechiefen," Dobro clarified.

A spark of recognition lit Arliss's face. "A feechie," he said knowingly. Now he understood why Dobro looked and talked so peculiar.

"That's right," Dobro said. "I'm a natural-born feechie, but I figured it was time I give civilizin' a try."

Arliss looked at Aidan. "We been speculating whether you'd bring feechies with you when you come back."

"Well, one feechie," Aidan began, "and only because he wouldn't take no for an answer."

But Arliss couldn't contain himself any longer. He was too excited to listen to Aidan's explanation. "Wait till I tell the boys," he said, then he turned and sprinted up the canyon.

Aidan turned to Dobro. "If you want to pass yourself off as a civilizer, you've got to stop talking about the Feechiefen."

"And you need to know about shaking hands," Percy added.

"Shaky hands?" Dobro said. "No, thank you. My hands is good and steady, and I aim to keep them that way, whether I'm feechified or civilized."

"No, Dobro, shaking hands—it's a civilizer greeting. It's what we do instead of head butting. If somebody reaches a hand out like this"—Percy extended his right hand—"you grip it nice and firm and give it a shake. Try it."

Dobro grabbed Percy's hand and began to shake it violently back and forth, like a terrier shaking a rat.

"No, Dobro, not that way," Percy yelled, wrenching his hand out of Dobro's powerful grip. "You're not supposed to shake the other fellow's armbone to jelly. Watch how Aidan and I do it."

But Aidan and Percy never gave their handshaking demonstration. Just then Errol appeared from around the nearest bend in the canyon.

He was running toward the three travelers, and running surprisingly well for a white-haired man in his sixties. Just behind him were Jasper and Brennus. Aidan ran to embrace his father. The old man's cheeks were wet with joyful tears, and he could barely speak—couldn't, in fact, say anything but Aidan's name over and over.

Aidan embraced Brennus and Jasper with all the affection of a long-lost brother, and there were more tears of joy all around. Dobro was so affected by the scene that he, too, began to cry sloppily and loudly.

"Father, this is Dobro Turtlebane," Aidan began, "the feechie friend I have told you about."

"You are very welcome to Sinking Canyons, Dobro," Errol said, extending his right hand. Aidan was afraid for a moment that Dobro would seize his father's hand and shake his arm out of its socket, but instead he fell on Errol's neck and buried his face in the older man's shoulder. "Thank you for them kind words, Mr. Errol," he sobbed. "Any daddy of Aidan's is a daddy of mine. And I ain't had no daddy since the gator down at Devil's Elbow knocked mine out'n a flatboat and et him—and me no more'n a yearling at the time."

Percy continued the introductions. "Dobro, this is Brennus, our eldest brother, and Jasper, my twin." Dobro seized both brothers in a single hug and cried again.

Aidan looked beyond his father and brothers and for the first time realized how many men were living in Sinking Canyons. There must have been sixty or seventy of them, all keeping their distance out of respect for the family reunion. Errol noticed the look of astonishment on Aidan's face. "Our band of outlaws," he said, throwing his thumb over his shoulder. "Didn't Percy tell you?"

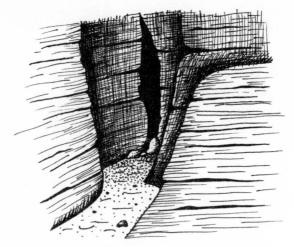

Chapter Eleven

Introductions

P ercy didn't tell me there were so many!" Aidan recognized many of the men, but nearly half were strangers to him. "Who are they?" he asked.

Errol led his sons and Dobro to the clusters of men who had been watching them. "You remember the Greasy Cave boys," he said.

"Of course," Aidan answered. "We saw Arliss before. Ernest. Cedric. Clayton." He shook hands with each in turn. "And Gustus, the foreman." Gustus gave a toothy grin, then broke into an energetic but tuneless version of the song Aidan had composed for the miner-scouts the night they went down to the caverns beneath Bonifay Plain:

Oh, the miners brave of Greasy Cave,
They did not think it odd
To make their way beneath the clay,
Where human foot had never trod.

The rest of the miners joined on the chorus, improving it only slightly:
Fol de rol de rol de fol de rol de rol
De fol de rol de fiddely fol de rol.

"King Darrow got it in his head that you was hiding out in the mines at Greasy Cave," Gustus said. "Thought your old friends was protecting you, which we would have, if ever you had asked us. So he outlawed us."

"Every last one of us," Cedric added.

"Your pap got wind of the outlawing and sent Brennus to fetch those of us what might want to hide out in Sinking Canyons," Gustus continued. "All five of us from the Bonifay adventure come along, plus another eight." He gestured at a group of men, short and stocky like the rest of the Greasy Cave boys, who waved bashfully at Aidan.

"Their skills have been invaluable here in the canyons," Errol remarked. "I don't know how we would have gotten along without them.

"And then there are the Last Campers." Errol gestured toward a group of men all clad in buckskin.

"Massey. Floyd." Aidan shook the men's hands vigorously. "Do you still do any timber rafting? Hugh. Isom. Big Haze. Little Haze. Chaney. Burl. Cooky, are you cooking for the men here too?"

"Yeah," the old cook grumbled. "Not that nobody appreciates all the trouble I go to. And it ain't easy feeding sixty folks,"—he gestured at Aidan and Dobro—"now sixty-two folks, on the stringy deer and skinny possum what live around here."

"Same old Cooky," Aidan smiled. "Same old grouchy Cooky."

"We got outlawed for 'aiding and abetting a enemy of the king,'" said Massey. "You being the enemy of the king, don't you know. Just imagine it: I don't even know what 'aiding and abetting' means, but here I am guilty of it. Shows you never do know. But if I got to be outlawed for something, I like the sound of 'aiding and abetting.' It's a sight better than cattle rustling or poaching."

"Jasper come to fetch us when your pa heard we was outlaws," said Floyd. "And I don't mind telling you it's a heap more fun being in a band of outlaws than outlawing alone."

"These boys have kept us in meat since they got here," Errol added. "They can always find us a deer or a wild hog."

"But nary a alligator," Massey remarked wistfully.

Errol gestured toward two older men whom Aidan knew very well. "King Darrow outlawed Lord Cleland and Lord Aethelbert and their sons when they protested our being outlawed. We all came to Sinking Canyons together two years ago, along with Ebbe and the field hands." Ebbe, the stuffy old house servant, bowed to Aidan. He didn't seem quite so stuffy out here in the wilderness, though his tunic was remarkably well kept. Aidan shook hands with the six field hands he had known all his life.

A lot of familiar faces. But there were still plenty of faces Aidan had never seen before. He was surprised to see a dozen men wearing the same standard-issue blue army tunics he, Percy, and Dobro wore. "Soldiers," Errol explained. "Scouts, actually. King Darrow sent a half dozen men to track us in the canyons, and when they found us . . ."

"When you found us, you mean," laughed one of the scouts.

"When we found them, then," Errol smiled, "they decided that life among outlaws was better than life in King Darrow's army."

But that accounted for only half of the soldiers in the group. "Where did the other half dozen come from?" Aidan asked.

"They're the search party," Errol said, smiling. "The ones King Darrow sent out to find the first party."

"And they deserted too?" Aidan asked.

Errol's smile faded. "These men are not deserters. They are men of honor. Understand this, Aidan, and do not doubt it: We remain King Darrow's most loyal subjects. It would have been no loyalty to King

Darrow if these soldiers had handed us over to certain death, leaving only time-servers and flatterers in Darrow's service. No, by disobeying King Darrow's orders these men have done him a great service, whether the king knows it or not."

Aidan gave his father a long and watchful look. Errol had always taken a dim view of deserters, had always insisted on unswerving obedience to the king. Was this the same father he had always known, now saying that disobedience to the king was service to the king? Yes, things had changed in the years Aidan had been away.

"And who are they?" Aidan asked, pointing at a tight knot of eight or ten men gathered apart from the rest of the group and talking among themselves.

Errol paused before speaking. "They joined us only recently. I don't know most of their names. They're outlaws like us."

"They may be outlaws," Jasper muttered, "but they're not like us."

Errol gave his son a sharp look. He obviously didn't intend to speak candidly in the hearing of the whole group. "Marvin," Errol called toward the group. "You and the boys come say hello to my son Aidan."

Marvin was a mountain of a man. His face was as round as the full moon and pocked like the moon too. It bulged against a massive quid of tobacco in his left cheek. He was bald on top, with long, thin hair straggling down the back of his neck. He moved slowly, deliberately toward Aidan, but his eyes were quick. He offered what he meant for a smile. It looked more like a sneer; it showed his big, brown-stained teeth.

Towering over Aidan, Marvin extended a hand. Aidan reached out his own hand to shake; sausage-thick fingers wrapped around it and squeezed with a crushing force that nearly brought tears to Aidan's eyes. "I'm Marvin," the big man said. He pointed at the ragtag group of dirty men he had just come from. "This here's the boys."

He looked at Aidan with an appraising eye and gave a snort that suggested he was none too impressed. "Ain't you supposed to be the Wilderking or something?" Two or three of his cronies snickered.

Aidan didn't know how to respond to Marvin's remark, so he didn't respond at all. Dobro, meanwhile, was admiring the long hair that draped down the back of Marvin's neck. It was the most feechiefied haircut he had seen on a civilizer, and he felt an immediate connection.

Marvin noticed him staring. "What are you looking at, Snaggletooth?" he snarled.

"I was just likin' your hairdo," Dobro said. "Ain't a lot of civilizers got that much style."

Marvin squinted at Dobro, not sure whether or not this scrawny fellow was making fun of him. "Coming from a feller as ugly as you, I don't know how to take that."

Dobro shrugged. "Take it however you want to take it. It don't make me no never mind."

Marvin found himself getting annoyed at the nonchalant attitude of this ugly runt, who obviously wasn't intimidated by him. "Say, boy," he said, looking intently at Dobro, "how'd you get so ugly?"

"I reckon he's a feechie," said one of Marvin's followers. "Ain't I always said the Wilderking would come back with feechies?"

Dobro nodded at Marvin. "He got it right. I might look like a civilizer—scrubbed pink and with my mane lopped off—but I'm feechie born and bred." There was nothing civilized about the green smile he directed at Marvin, or the acrid breath he exhaled in a self-satisfied sigh.

"Well, I don't believe in feechiefolks," Marvin insisted. "And if I did, I don't reckon I'd think too highly of them." He squirted a jet of tobacco juice on the ground in front of Dobro's bare feet and wiped his thumb across his grinning lips.

Dobro eyed Marvin, trying to figure out what was the proper civilizer response to such a challenge. He figured he couldn't go wrong if he responded in kind, so he worked up a nice, foamy glob of spit and let it fly right between the big man's boots.

Marvin flew into a rage. He raised a huge fist and brought it down like a sledge hammer. It surely would have cracked Dobro's skull if it had connected, but the feechie was too quick for him. He scrambled between Marvin's legs and scurried up his back. Dobro reached one arm around the big man's neck in a choke hold. His free thumb he stuck in Marvin's eye. Marvin staggered, roared, and rained blows on Dobro, but he couldn't do any real damage to the wiry feechie. When Dobro reared back and butted the back of Marvin's head, the big man crumpled to the ground in a senseless heap.

Dobro was feeling a little woozy himself. Butting Marvin's massive head was very much like butting a tree. When Marvin's followers made a circle around him, Dobro was a little unsteady on his feet. But his mouth was still working fine. "I weigh 'bout 125 when I'm friendly," he shouted, "But now I'm angrified, I weigh about seven hundred!"

Marvin's gang all raised their fists and made menacing faces, but none of them wanted to be the first to take on the wild man who had felled their leader. "I can pick the ticks off'n all you boys," Dobro roared. "All at once or one at a time, whichever suits you better."

Marvin's boys seemed relieved when Errol pushed through them and grabbed the raging feechie by the shoulders. "Enough," the old man yelled, barely able to suppress a smile. "That's probably enough introductions for one day."

With much effort, Marvin's men dragged their leader to the shady spot and revived him with stream water. The other men surrounded Dobro; they were fascinated by him—a real-live feechie—and awed at his efficient whipping of a man so much larger than himself. Dobro basked in their admiration and kept them royally entertained with his peculiar observations about civilizer life and customs.

The men would have surrounded Aidan, of course, except his father had whisked him away immediately after he had settled Dobro.

"Who are those people?" Aidan asked as father and son walked up the canyon toward the camp and sleeping quarters. "Marvin and his gang? Where did they come from?"

"I'm not sure where they came from," Errol answered. "They came to the canyons a couple of months ago, claiming to be on the run from King Darrow, so we took them in. That was Aethelbert's idea—thought they would be good fellows to have on our side in a fight." Errol shook his head. "They were on their best behavior for a while, but I've about decided they're just common criminals."

"Or spies?" Aidan asked.

"I've considered that," Errol said, "but I don't think so. I'm not sure they've got enough sense to make spies."

"Maybe not," Aidan agreed. "But that Marvin may not be as stupid as he looks."

"Yes, Marvin's trouble. He's trouble if he stays, and he may be more trouble if we send him away."

"Because he knows we're in Sinking Canyons," Aidan said.

"Actually, I'm starting to think everybody in Corenwald knows we're in Sinking Canyons. King Darrow most certainly knows. The problem is that Marvin and his crowd know where most of our hiding places are." They walked past a wide, deep place in the canyon stream. "The miners dug that," Errol remarked. "It's where we do our washing. Looks natural, doesn't it?"

He pointed to a crevice in the side of the canyon, no different from hundreds of cracks in the canyon wall. "This is our main hideout and storage area," he said.

Aidan followed his father through the crack in the wall. It was so narrow they couldn't walk through side by side. But just a few steps in, beyond the first turn, the little crack broadened into a rounded tunnel, obviously dug by human hands. "This is the miners' work again," Errol said, his voice echoing against the walls.

It wasn't, properly speaking, a tunnel, but a widening of the crevice, which continued above their heads all the way up to the canyon rim and to the sunlight above. They continued deeper into the canyon wall until the tunnel opened into quite a large, round room. A shaft of sunlight made its way a hundred feet down from the canyon rim to illuminate the place. A few wisps of smoke curled up from a banked fire in the center of the room and slithered up the crevice as if it were a chimney. It was all strangely beautiful.

Errol pointed up into the sunlight. "Sometimes when we have been to the villages to trade, we lower supplies down by ropes.

"This crevice is actually the beginning of a new branch of the canyon. As years go by, it will open more and more. Someday this won't be much of a hiding place. But surely we will have no need of a hiding place by then. For now, it serves just fine."

Errol pointed at five tunnel entrances that opened onto the large chamber, joining like spokes on a hub. "Sleeping chambers and storage rooms," he explained.

"The miners dug all this?" Aidan asked. "How long did it take?"

"Not as long as you'd think," Errol answered. "The rest of us couldn't carry out the sand nearly as quickly as they could dig it. They're used to chipping their way through rock. This sand and clay is child's play for them."

Aidan looked up at the sliver of sky visible through the crack in the ceiling. "Doesn't the rain get in here?"

"In here, yes," Errol said. "But not up there." He pointed up one of the tunnels. He picked up one of the pine knot torches that lay stacked in piles beside the wall and poked it around in the banked fire until it lit. "Follow me," he said, and he stooped to walk up the tunnel.

"Even if it floods," Errol explained, "these chambers stay dry. The tunnels are dug on an upward slope." The sloping tunnel reached a plateau, from which connected three chambers. "You and Dobro will sleep here on the left with your brothers and me." Errol pointed to the chamber on the right. "Here are Marvin and the boys, where I can keep a close eye on them. And there at the end of the tunnel, a provisioning room." He held his torch in the room to show Aidan great bags of flour, rice, and dried beans stacked in neat rows.

It was an impressive feat of engineering and effort. But it was a long way from the life Aidan felt his father deserved. "Father, I'm sorry," he said. "This is all my fault—your being outlawed, your living in a hole in the ground."

"It's not your fault, Aidan," Errol said. "You do what you have to do. We all do. Life in the canyons isn't what I had expected, but it's a very good life in its way.

"Just a few years ago, this place seemed like alien soil, no more like Corenwald than the moon. But now it feels as if this is the only Corenwald that's left. For us, the land of the free and true has shrunk down to this one barren, godforsaken spot. Here we live free and true. We live like Corenwalders, something we couldn't do anymore in the Corenwald we used to know. Here, among us outlaws, Corenwald survives."

Chapter Twelve

Floodwaters

The men were telling stories by the fire one breezy afternoon when the storm came. "My Uncle Armand was the finest feller you'll ever meet," began Isom, "but, man, was he ugly."

Little Haze had heard this tale many times at Last Camp, but nevertheless he obligingly asked Isom the question the old deer hunter was hoping someone would ask: "How ugly was he, Isom?"

Isom winked his thanks to Little Haze over the fire. "Poor Armand. Before he married Aunt Flossie, she'd only let him come courting after dark, and even then she'd only let him come as far as the porch. The porch lantern was broke, don't you see."

"That's some kind of ugly, if your sweetie can't even stand to look at you," remarked one of the Greasy Cave boys.

"That ain't the half of it," Isom continued. "Uncle Armand was cutting across Flossie's pasture one day on his way to the big road—her daddy's farm was next door to his, don't you see—and he heard the sound of smacking and smooching behind a big bank of blackberry bushes. Armand was curious by nature, and he wasn't in no particular hurry, so he peeped around the bush and seen Flossie kissing her milk cow square on the mouth. Armand hollers, 'Flossie, what ails you? Why you smooching a milk cow?' Flossie felt a little bashful, but she could tell Armand wasn't going nowhere till he had a answer. She told him, 'Sugar, I knowed you was going to want to kiss me after we got married. I'm just working up my gumption.'"

The crowd roared at that, which encouraged Isom to press on. "Being ugly's how Armand made his living, don't you see."

Percy was fascinated. "How can a fellow make a living by being ugly?"

"When folks around the village was sitting down for supper, he'd show up," Isom explained, "and he was so astonishing ugly, they'd throw biscuits at him, chicken legs, whatever they had to hand, trying to scare him off. On a good day he'd catch a whole roast beef to carry home for Aunt Flossie and them ugly babies of theirs. One time he come home with the prettiest silver tea set you ever saw."

"It's always a pleasure to hear about folks making the most of their God-given abilities," Massey observed. This philosophical remark was hardly out of the old alligator hunter's mouth when a tremendous clap of thunder shattered the air and the rain began—not gradually building in intensity but driven in sheets by the wind, as suddenly and almost as violently as the thunder itself.

The men ran for the shelter of their hiding crevice and the tunnels the miners designed for just such an emergency as this. One at a time they pushed through the narrow opening, pelted not merely by rain, but also by the mud that glanced off the canyon walls. Within seconds the floor of the entry tunnel was a fast-moving creek well over the men's ankles; for the rain that fell on a wide swath of the plain above funneled into this crevice and tumbled down from the canyon rim a hundred feet in a rushing cataract, shooting down the tunnel to join the growing torrent that had been the braided stream.

The rain kept coming unabated. The men had to push against a growing current to get to the main chamber and the safety of the tunnels. The water was soon shin high; everyone's boots were full of water, and the wet clay made for terrible footing. Twice men slipped and bowled down three or four men behind them before they could get to their feet again.

Aidan and Dobro were at the back of the line, the anchor and last defense for anyone in danger of being swept into the current that raged in the main canyon. Dobro himself slipped once, his bare toes losing their purchase when he stepped in clay. But Aidan caught him by the tunic as he swept past and was somehow able to keep his own footing.

"I know you've had a hankering to swim, Dobro," Aidan shouted over the rushing of water, "but this isn't a good time!"

A flash of lightning lit Dobro's terrified face. "Time to leave these neighborhoods!" he yelled.

The echoing roar was deafening in the main chamber, where the waterfall from the surface pounded against the ground and splattered mud in every direction. Aidan's ears were ringing as he struggled to climb into the tunnel that led to the Errolsons' sleeping chamber. The tunnel was a slippery slope, but at least there was no current to contend with after they left the main chamber.

When Aidan and Dobro reached their chamber, there was much rejoicing. Errol, Brennus, Jasper, and Percy were all safe and all greatly relieved to see Aidan and Dobro unhurt. On the other side of the tunnel, Marvin and his gang were safe and sound, though bedraggled.

The storm continued through the night. It was a night of much anxiety, for even if all fifteen people in the Errolsons' tunnel were accounted for, they had no way of knowing how things stood in the other tunnels. Then there was always the possibility the water could rise high enough to close the tunnel entrance and seal off their supply of air. It seemed unlikely, and if it happened, it was more unlikely they would consume all the air in the tunnel before the waters receded. Even so, the possibility, however remote, of suffocating in the company of Marvin and his boys made Aidan feel queasy.

"We've done all we can do," Errol said. "We are in the hands of the living God." Then he lay down on his pallet and went to sleep. His sons and Dobro, on the other hand, were unable to sleep and didn't even try.

Meanwhile, Marvin and the boys were having a prayer meeting out in the tunnel, where the water continued to creep higher and higher. No one had ever known them to pray before, even at mealtimes, but there they were, praying loudly and earnestly, making deals with God, promising to behave themselves if only God would deliver them. Their prayers grew louder and more desperate the higher the waters rose. Marvin stood at the very edge of the water and commanded it in the name of the living God to come no farther. But by the time he opened his eyes after his lengthy prayer, his toes were under water.

Aidan tapped Marvin on the shoulder. "Um, Marvin," he began, "I think you boys have the right idea, of course, but do you think you could pray a little more quietly? Father is trying to sleep."

Marvin's eyes burned with righteous indignation. "I thought your pap was a man of faith. Why ain't he out here praying with us instead of sleeping?"

Aidan smiled. "Father is a man of faith. That's why he can sleep on a night like this. He prayed for an hour or more this morning, just like every morning, while you were still snoring. He prayed for you by name, in fact, Marvin. I heard him. Father's been praying all day. And now he's resting in the mercy of the living God."

Marvin looked back at the rising water. "Aw, forget it," he said and stalked back toward his sleeping quarters, his followers right behind him.

"I don't mean to discourage your praying," Aidan called behind him.

Marvin waved a hand behind him. "It ain't working anyway."

‡ ‡ ‡

In the morning a gray light filtered up the tunnels, but the roar of the waterfall in the main chamber continued as strong as ever. The water had climbed farther up the tunnel in the dark hours of the morning. Were it to rise another foot, it would flood the sleeping chambers and spoil the foodstuffs in the storage room.

The men were restacking bags of flour against that possibility when they noticed the waterfall's roar had lessened. The rain had stopped, and it was only a matter of minutes before most of the surface water funneling into the crevice had run its course. The water in the tunnel began to recede and the waterfall, while still much stronger than a trickle, was nothing like the torrent that had thundered all night long.

In less than an hour, the water was gone from the tunnels. By the time another half hour had passed, the water coursing along the crevice floor had subsided enough for the men to step out into the sunshine that flooded the floor of the main chamber. Everyone was safe. All thirteen miners, nine hunters, twelve soldiers, six field hands, seven noblemen, and, of course, the fifteen men in the Errolsons' tunnel were accounted for. The men offered up prayers of praise and thanks-giving.

The stream in the main canyon was still raging—a muddy, milky, reddish torrent. From the markings on the canyon walls, it was obvious the water had already fallen several feet.

"If the rain don't come back—and it don't look like it will—this creek'll be within a foot of normal by this afternoon," Gustus observed. "And we can start work on the main chamber."

The pounding water had dug a broad bowl in the soft dirt of the crevice floor. Even when the last of the surface water had flowed through and out to the main channel, a little pond, a foot and a half deep, would remain in the chamber to grow stagnant and breed mosquitoes if the men didn't do something about it.

The miners fell to the work with great enthusi-asm—digging and grading, filling and scraping. They were proud of their work, proud of their expertise, proud when their comrades said they didn't know what they would do without them, because they knew it was true. That feeling of being indispensable wasn't one they got very often when they were toil-ing in the mines at Greasy Cave. In their workaday world, amid the dangers they faced daily in the mines, they felt very dispensable. The fact that they mostly looked alike—short, stocky, bearded—only added to the sense of interchangeability. Everybody in Greasy Cave could swing a pickax, and if a miner didn't show up at the mines one day, the boss would surely find somebody else who would, and he would never miss a lick.

But here in Sinking Canyons, the Greasy Cave boys were heroes, just as they had been at Bonifay. Their tunnels had saved the lives of their comrades. Now they were in charge of the cleanup, organizing the others (civilians, as they had come to think of non-miners) into bucket brigades and telling them what to do and how to do it.

The others were happy to follow the miners' leadership—most of them anyway. Marvin and his gang grumbled all afternoon and dropped their buckets on every other pass and sometimes wandered off from the work a half hour at a time.

After a cold and early supper, Gustus announced, "Boys, we still got a couple hours' daylight left. What say we finish up this job so we don't have to fool with it tomorrow?"

Everyone's back was aching from the day's work. But the men did like the idea of not having to return to the work a second day, so they stood, stretched, and prepared to go back to the bucket brigade.

They all stopped, however, at the booming voice of Marvin echoing on the canyon walls. "Some band of outlaws this is!" He threw his head back and laughed. "Toting buckets of sand! Getting bossed by a bunch of miners!" He pointed a finger at the miners gathered around Gustus. "I've took all the orders I aim to take from a bunch of stoop-backed gravel scratchers."

Ernest gave it back to Marvin. "I didn't hear no complaints about gravel scratchers when you was safe and dry last night in the tunnels we dug!"

Marvin waved at the air as if swatting away a bothersome fly. The rest of the miners now stepped up beside Ernest, across from Marvin's gang, who fanned out to face them. The miners gripped their pickaxes and shovels. From the looks on their faces, it appeared they were ready to use them.

But Errol and his four sons stepped into the corridor between the two lines of men. The old man stood mere inches away from Marvin. The purple vein had appeared on his forehead. He spoke calmly but with unquestionable authority. "No one is keeping you here, Marvin. Leave anytime you wish. But if you mean to use our shelter and eat our food, you will join us in our work."

Marvin snorted. "It'll be dark in an hour. The water's still high. We can't leave now."

Errol grabbed a bucket from one of the miners and shoved it into Marvin's belly. "Then get to work," he ordered, stalking off to join the bucket brigade himself.

Chapter Thirteen

A Discovery

idan lay awake most of that night, half-expecting trouble from Marvin and his boys. He finally fell asleep a couple of hours before dawn, and when he awoke, Marvin's gang was gone. Cooky had seen the group leave while he was trying to light the breakfast fire in the predawn darkness.

Never had a day seemed fresher. Marvin's departure was like a shadow lifting. The morning sun glistened off the stream, now only a little higher than normal. The birds that had spent the previous day drying out sang joyously in celebration of the new day.

After breakfast Aidan joined Jasper on a walk down the canyon. "The canyon changes after every rainstorm," Jasper explained. "And the storm we just had was the biggest one we've had since we've been here. Look, this is what I'm talking about." He pointed at a spot where the water flowed over flat sand.

"Looks like any other spot on the canyon floor," Aidan said, not sure what point Jasper was making.

"But it didn't two days ago," Jasper said. "This was the wash hole. Remember those two willow trees right there? The ones where we always hang clothes to dry?"

"You're right," Aidan said, looking at the two big trees, then back down at the stream. "But that was a pretty big pool."

"Took the miners most of a week to dig it," Jasper agreed. "But it probably took only a few minutes for the flood to fill it back in." He pointed up the canyon. "The sand and clay that washed down the stream and probably some from up there at the canyon rim got dumped into the pool here until it filled up."

Jasper pointed at a smooth mound across the way. "Remember the tower that used to stand there? It must have crumbled away and washed downstream."

"Amazing," Aidan said. "So the storm tears down the high spots and fills in the low spots?"

"Sort of," Jasper answered, "Sometimes it makes low spots lower, digging a little furrow into a big trench. Sometimes part of a wall crumbles away and leaves a new tower or chimney that wasn't there before. The only thing you can be sure of is that dirt is going to move around. After a rain like this one, some spots get buried in sand and clay, and some spots get unburied. No rhyme or reason to it, as far as I can make out."

Aidan pointed up at a pine tree on the very edge of the canyon. It was the one he had noticed when he first came here, with its roots reaching out into the air. "I remember that tree," he said. "It used to have a neighbor. Do you remember? It hung upside down by the roots, just a few feet from that tree."

"It's gone now," Jasper observed. "The storm must have been too much for it."

"Wonder where it is now," said Aidan. "Maybe floating down the Eechihoolee by now, on its way to the ocean."

"Or it might be out here somewhere. Likely it's buried in the sand," said Jasper.

Aidan walked toward the canyon wall where the tree had hung, curious to see if it was on the canyon floor. He saw no sign of the tree, but he did see something else that caught his eye. "Hey, Jasper," he called. "Come over here. What does this look like to you?"

Jasper knelt beside him in the wet sand and examined the flat, brittle piece of wood Aidan handed him. It was a little bigger than a man's hand. A whole row of identical pieces peeked out of the sand like a row of teeth.

"It looks like a shingle to me," Jasper said.

"That's what I thought," Aidan agreed. From his side pouch he pulled out a flat digging rock, a leftover from his Feechiefen days, and began digging around the shingles. They were attached to a wide plank, a piece of roof decking, no doubt. There was a second row of shingles nailed just below the first.

"Do you suppose a piece of roof from an old barn washed down here from a nearby farm?" Aidan asked.

Jasper gazed up at the canyon rim. "The nearest farm I know of is almost ten leagues away. That was a powerful storm, but I don't see how surface water—or really anything less than a river—could carry something this big for ten leagues." He thought on it a little more. "And besides, when was the last time you saw a shingled roof in this part of Corenwald? All the roofs around here are reed thatch or palmetto thatch."

"You're right," Aidan said. "This is like a roof you might see in the Hill Country."

"Or the old country." Jasper's brow crinkled. "So how did it get here?"

Aidan dug again with his rock. But even in the wet sand he couldn't make enough progress to suit Jasper, who was growing more perplexed and more excited about their discovery. "I'm going to get the miners," he announced. "They'll have it dug out in no time."

‡ ‡ ‡

An hour's digging by the miners produced impressive results. They dug out the decking plank within ten minutes of arriving on the scene. Then they found two more shingled planks and a pair of massive roof timbers, almost as big as squared-off trees.

Except for those on sentry duty, every man in the camp came to watch the digging and debate about the findings. Everyone agreed the planks and timbers hadn't been washed down by the flood of two days earlier. They were buried too deeply for that. This flood must have just washed away the sand that had buried the planks and timbers many years earlier. But that didn't explain how they got there in the first place.

One of the soldiers proposed that pirates or criminals had built a house in the canyon for a hideout and a flood had destroyed it. But in a canyon full of natural hideouts, it seemed unlikely that anyone would actually build a house to hide in.

Someone else suggested that the house may have overhung the canyon at one time and fallen into the canyon just as the pine tree had fallen during the storm. But again, who would be fool enough to build a house overlooking Sinking Canyons? The place got its very name from the rim constantly sinking down to the canyon floor.

While the debate continued, the miners continued digging. Soon they made another discovery. Digging out the deeper end of one of the roof timbers, Clayton's shovel clanged against something metal. Soon he had uncovered a thickly corroded plate of curved iron. The field hands were the first to recognize it as a plow blade.

"Oh, Mama," Dobro moaned. "Oh, Mama, if you only knew what your boy been messing up with!"

Everyone stopped to stare at the feechie, who wrung his hands in genuine distress.

"What is the matter with you, Dobro?" Aidan asked.

Dobro was breathing fast, trying to regain his composure. "Ain't but three things my mama especially tolt me was bad luck to mess up with—three things ain't no feechie supposed to mess up with—and here I am messing up with all three at the same time."

"What in the world are you talking about?" asked Arliss.

Dobro held up his index finger. "One, civilizers. I don't mean to hurt nobody's feelings, but you folks is bad luck." He held up two fingers. "Two, Sinking Canyons. Feechiefolks go wherever they want to go on this island, 'cept Sinking Canyons and places that got civilizers. Here I stand in the middle of Sinking Canyons with a crowd of civilizers. And now the next thing to turn up is the very worst luck in the round world: a cold-shiny plow!" He looked as if he might start crying. "Any cold-shiny's bad luck for feechiefolks, of course, but a cold-shiny plow's the worst bad luck of all."

"What's so awful about a cold-shiny plow?" Percy asked.

Dobro didn't seem to have heard the question. But he closed his eyes and launched into a feechie sadballad:

Oh, Veezo, you is ruint,
Covered by the clay.

With choppin' and plowin'
You tore up the ground
And now it's washed away.

Oh, Veezo, you is ruint,
Buried in the sand.
The world caved in,
And you and your kin
Was swallowed by the land.

Oh, Veezo, you is ruint,
And all your folks is gone.
They took to the bogs,
Now your horses and hogs
Got to make it on their own.

Oh, Veezo, you is ruint,
Underneath the ground.
Your cold-shiny's rusted,
Your cabins is busted.
They'll never more be found.

"It's all right there in the feechie lore," Dobro explained. "All about Veezo and his magical cold-shiny plow." He wiped away a tear of self-pity. "In the old times, way before civilizers come to Corenwald, feechiefolks was farmers and villagers, just like you. And the biggest feechie farmer of them all was a feller named Veezo. And weren't he a greedisome rascal! He farmed more land than any other man on the island, but his feelings was hurt because it weren't enough for him.

"He was settin' in his yard one evening with his lips pooched out when *poof!* A yard fairy turnt up."

"A what?" Big Haze asked.

"A yard fairy—you know, the kind of fairy lives in folkses' yards. And the yard fairy says 'Veezo, how come your lips is pooched out?'

"Veezo says, 'My feelin's is hurt because I ain't got enough land to plow. I plow all the land a man and a mule can plow, but it ain't enough.'

"The fairy says, 'I see. If you already plowing all the ground a man and a mule can plow, what you need is a magical cold-shiny plow.' And *poof!* There one is, just as shiny and pretty a thing as Veezo ever seen. His eyes gets real big, account of he's so greedi-some.

"Then the fairy says, 'Just don't plow too long a furrow.'

"Veezo's so wondrous he almost don't hear the fairy's warnin', but finally he pulls his eyes off'n that cold-shiny plow long enough to ask, 'How long is too long a furrow?' But the fairy's gone.

"Next day, Veezo commences to plowin', and he plows the prettiest ankle-deep furrow long enough to grow corn for the whole neighborhood. He figures that must be long enough a furrow, and he ought to turn around, but then he figures he might want a pun-kin patch too. So he given his mule a swat, and on they go another piece. Veezo don't even notice now that his magical cold-shiny plow's cuttin' a furrow knee-deep and two foot wide.

"He's about to turn his mule around, but then he figures some watermelons might be just the thing. So he gives his mule another swat, and on they go another piece. He don't notice that his magical cold-shiny plow is diggin' a furrow shoulder high and ten foot across.

"Veezo was just about to turn that mule around when he got a hankerin' for onions and decided he'd plow up a onion patch. He give his mule a swat and on they go. He didn't know he was plowin' right through his own yard because his furrow was deeper than his head and fifty foot wide! He just kept on plowin', happy as a jaybird, and his cabin dropped into the furrow, then his barns dropped in the furrow, and finally the clay just tumbled in on top of Veezo and buried him and his magical cold-shiny plow too.

"And that's why feechies is swamp folks, forest folks. Veezo's neighbors seen what come of farmin', and they takened to the woods where they could get their nourishment without cuttin' furrows with no cold-shiny plow."

Dobro looked solemnly at his hearers. "And the moral of the story is: *Don't go messin' up with cold-shiny plows.*"

"I thought the moral was don't go messin' up with yard fairies," Percy chimed in.

But Dobro paid him no mind.

"Hey, Dobro," Percy teased, "you don't suppose that's Veezo's cabin and magical plow we found, do you?"

Dobro looked thoughtfully into the hole the miners had dug. "I reckon that's as good a explanation as anything you civilizers has come up with."

Chapter Fourteen

New Recruits

Hiding out was dull work. Perhaps that was why the men at Sinking Canyons took such an interest in Jasper's archaeological dig. It gave them something to do, something to talk about, a mystery to figure out. They held lengthy debates over whether it made more sense to dig shallow over a broad area, or more deeply in a tighter, focused area. Many of the men kept their own catalogs of the objects found at the diggings, separate from the official record kept by Jasper, who hoped to donate his work to the university in Tambluff as soon as the Errolsons returned to Corenwalder society.

Not that there were many findings to record. They found more timbers and some floorboards they believed came from a separate building. They also found a brass pot and a rusted pair of iron tongs wedged between a couple of timbers. But for the most part, it appeared the smaller items that had been in those buildings at one time—tools, cooking utensils, clothing, furniture, all those everyday objects that told the story of a people's way of life—had disappeared, probably washed away through the years. Only the big timbers and the iron plow had the heft to stand their ground and be buried in the sand, then be uncovered again so many years later.

It was the plow that had everyone flummoxed. Maybe, just maybe, a man would have reason to build a house here in the Clay Wastes. Maybe he was a hermit. But not even a hermit would try to farm this land, not when he could go anyplace else on the island and make a better crop with a lot less effort.

Some of the miners had floated a theory that the Eechihoolee River once flowed through the canyons and had changed course. A river at flood stage could carry timbers a good long way. After all, that was how the timber rafters got their logs from the forests to the seaports. That still didn't explain how the iron plow blade got there. And besides, the Eechihoolee wasn't all that close. If it had changed course in the last hundred years since Corenwald had been settled, surely somebody would have known something about it.

Work in the diggings was going a little more slowly than Jasper had hoped. Much of the miners' time was occupied with digging a new washing pool where the old one had been ruined, and when they finished with that, Errol had put them on a new tunneling project on the other side of the canyon.

Errol and Aidan were at the new hideout when Clifford, the on-duty sentry, ran up with news of approaching men.

"How many?" Errol asked.

"Eighty, maybe ninety," Clifford answered.

A look of concern crossed Errol's face. "Armed?" he asked.

"You might say that," Clifford answered. "Some have rusty old swords; some have clubs or staves."

"Horseback or on foot?"

"On the march. I guess you'd call it marching," Clifford answered. "Oh, I almost forgot. They're wearing some kind of uniform. Green tunics and black hats with egret feathers."

"Oh no," Aidan groaned. "Aidanites! They've found me!" Percy doubled over in a fit of laughter.

"Come, men," Errol urged. "Away from the tunnels. No sense letting our guests see where our hideout is."

The Aidanites were already in sight. They were tromping up either side of the braided stream—a good policy if they were trying to keep their boots dry, but a terrible policy if they needed to keep their location and movements secret. They left thousands of bootprints that wouldn't wash away until the next good creek rising.

Aidan intercepted the men near the new washing pool, his comrades behind him. Just as he feared, they were Hustingreen Militia, led by Milum, the red-bearded Aidanite they met outside of Hustingreen. Milum stood at attention and popped his right hand over his heart in salute. The rest of the Aidanites saluted, too, though not very crisply. Milum dropped to one knee in front of Aidan. "Your Majesty, the

Hustingreen Militia, reporting for training camp and at your service."

"Training camp?" Aidan barked. "This isn't a training camp. It's a hideout." He looked over his green-clad followers. "Though it's obviously not a very good hideout!" He waved the backs of his hands at them, the way he might shoo a dog. "Get on," he shouted. "Go home!" He stomped a foot, but the Aidanites just stared vacantly at him.

"But what about the other militias?" Milum asked. "We're supposed to help get everything ready for them."

Aidan felt his stomach tighten. He struggled to speak calmly. "What other militias?"

Milum chuckled at first, assuming that Aidan must be pulling his leg. Of course the Wilderking knew which militias. How could he not know? Soon he realized, however, his king in exile really didn't know the plan. "Why, all the militias," Milum said. "The Bluemoss Boys, the Middenmarsh Militia, the Eechihoolee Regulars, the Berrien Militia, the Mountain Screamers. And all the others. The rest of the Hustingreen force is only a couple of days behind us."

Aidan felt light-headed. "You can't . . ." he began. "We can't . . . You've got to go home." He looked to his father for help.

Errol pulled him aside. "Here's the thing, Aidan," he whispered. "These boys can cause us a lot more trouble back home than they can cause us here. At least here we can keep an eye on them. Let's hear more from this Milum before we send them away."

Aidan turned back toward the Hustingreen Militia. "Men," he intoned, "welcome to Sinking Canyons. You may fall out, pending further orders." He turned to Milum. "Captain, a word with you, please."

Milum joined Aidan and Errol in the shade of an overhanging cliff. The three men squatted and sat on their heels, as Corenwalder men often did when speaking of serious matters.

"Who told you there was an Aidanite training camp in Sinking Canyons?" Aidan asked.

"Lynwood, Your Majesty. Who else?"

"First," said Aidan, "you've got to stop calling me 'Your Majesty.' I'm not king. I'm not even king in exile. I'm Aidan Errolson. You clear on that?"

"Yes, Your Maj— Yes, Aidan."

"Good. Now, who's this Lynwood?"

The look on Milum's face was one of pure astonishment. "Lynwood Wertenson."

"I should have guessed," Errol mumbled. "That upstart merchant has never been a friend to Darrow."

"He's the chair of the Committee," Milum added by way of clarification, but that clarified nothing for Aidan.

"What committee?" Aidan asked.

"The Secret Committee for the Ascendancy of the Wilderking," said Milum. "They're the governing body for all the local Aidanite auxiliaries and militias."

"This Lynwood," Aidan asked, "he's sending all the Aidanite militias to Sinking Canyons?"

"Yes, sir."

"How many militiamen is that?"

"Three thousand, maybe four."

"And how does this committee know I'm in Sinking Canyons?"

Milum smiled. "Aidan, everybody in Corenwald knows you're in Sinking Canyons. Everybody in Corenwald knows you come out of the Feechiefen in the company of a feechie. Every villager in Corenwald knows the Wilderking Chant by heart and can explain what every line of it has to do with Aidan Errolson." He smiled. "Don't you see, Aidan? Corenwald is waiting for you to claim the throne. King Darrow has lost his grip on the kingdom. Discipline has broken down in the army. Corenwald needs you, Aidan. No disrespect, but it looks like you and maybe King Darrow are the only people in Corenwald who don't realize it."

Aidan could feel the blood rising to his face. He thought he saw the vein appear on his father's forehead as well. Did anyone's oath of loyalty to King Darrow count for anything? "That's enough treasonous talk for now," Aidan said sharply.

"No disrespect, sir," said Milum, realizing that the interview was over.

A long silence prevailed between father and son after Milum left. "He's right about King Darrow's army," Errol said at last. "You've heard it a hundred times from Ottis, Wimbric, Hamp, and all the soldiers who have been living with us in Sinking Canyons. They say what Milum said. Discipline has broken down completely."

Errol broke off and stared across the canyon at the militiamen who wandered around, not sure what to do next. "You can be sure the Pyrthens know how the army has frittered away resources and morale carrying out King Darrow's worst impulses. The Pyrthens' spies are everywhere. The amazing thing is they haven't invaded already." He pointed at the militiamen. "Three thousand men. Maybe four thousand. They want to be an army. We could train them into an army."

Aidan looked at his father with horror. Was he speaking treason too?

"Aidan, don't you understand? When the Pyrthens come again—and they will—those three thousand men may be the only army Corenwald has left. We couldn't defeat the Pyrthens in a pitched battle. But we could make them sorry they came. Hit-and-run attacks. Rearward attacks on their supply train, horse rustling . . ."

"Feechie warfare," Aidan said, beginning to catch his father's vision.

"That's right," said Errol, with growing excitement. "I'm an old warhorse, and this wouldn't normally be my style, but you make do with what you have. The Last Campers are the best archers I've ever seen. They can teach those villagers to shoot. Our twelve army scouts will make a good beginning to a reconnaissance force. And the miners can show the militiamen how to dig shelters for themselves in the canyon walls."

Errol put his hands on Aidan's shoulders and looked intently into his eyes. "Bayard the Truthspeaker isn't here, so I'll tell you this myself: Live the life that unfolds before you. A small army is coming to Sinking Canyons. They want to follow you. That's what is unfolding before you today. You didn't ask for it. You didn't seek it. You didn't want it. But here it is. These men mean to follow you. They need to follow you. Will you lead them?"

"I'm not their king," Aidan said.

The vein on Errol's forehead appeared again. "Stop making excuses, Aidan!" The vehemence of his father's response surprised Aidan. "I never said you were anybody's king," Errol continued. "I asked if you would lead these men. You're not a boy anymore. You're a man. Don't make any more excuses. Just tell me whether or not you will lead these men."

In that moment of challenge, in that moment of seeming conflict, Aidan felt the blessing of his father pass to him. "Yes, Father," he said, "I will lead them."

Errol nodded, pleased with his son's answer. "Good," he said. "And just because you're leading, that doesn't mean you can't follow too. Lord willing, you'll lead these men to follow King Darrow."

Chapter Fifteen

A History Lesson

ithin a week all the militias had arrived at Sinking Canyons—thirty-six hundred men from every corner of Corenwald. Some had military experience. Many had fought the Pyrthens at the Battle of Bonifay Plain six years earlier. Some had actually been with King Darrow's army at Last Camp when Aidan came out of the Feechiefen with Percy and Dobro.

They came with stories of a kingdom in disarray. The army had fallen apart in the weeks since King Darrow abandoned his invasion of the Feechiefen. The king rode back to Tambluff alone, leaving no orders for his officers. The men just wandered back home to resume the lives they had left when they were forcibly drafted into the army. A few soldiers, in the absence of leadership, had taken to looting, highway robbery, and other crimes.

Sinking Canyons could no longer be properly called a hideout. There was no way of concealing the presence of so many men, even in the maze of caves and crevices. It was unmistakably a military outpost. Aidan worked with his father, his brothers, and the noblemen, Aethelbert and Cleland, to organize the militias into more efficient fighting units. They worked on the basics of sword fighting and archery, drilled quite a bit on troop movements—flanking an enemy, orderly retreat, field signals. But most of their time was devoted to tasks that related specifically to the kind of battle they expected to be fighting. They studied the geography of Sinking Canyons, learning every crevice, every finger, every tower and chimney, every fold in the earth that might provide cover in combat. They reviewed plans for ambushes and for search-and-rescue operations. They worked on tracking techniques and habits of concealment—always walking up the braided stream whenever possible, sweeping away tracks with pine boughs after walking through soft sand. Dobro offered special seminars on feechie methods of camouflage.

But more than anything, the new recruits spent their time digging. Under the miners' guidance, they dug tunnel after tunnel for shelter and storage. They dug out hiding places; they dug out wells. On more than one occasion, they dug each other out after poorly dug tunnels caved in.

The old-timers—the original band of Sinking Canyons outlaws—didn't have as many tunnel-digging responsibilities as the new recruits. They maintained their interest in Jasper's archaeological dig.

One day, Arliss made a discovery at the diggings that set the whole camp abuzz. It had been days since anyone had found anything more interesting than splintered logs or pieces of broken crockery. Then Arliss noticed a small, shiny disc peeking out from a shovelful of sand he was about to toss on the discard heap. It was a silver coin in surprisingly good shape, considering it had been buried for many years. He immediately ran with it to Jasper, who was cataloguing their findings, seated at a small campaign table he had taken from his father's cave.

"Fascinating," said Jasper, admiring the bright silver. Then his eyes grew wide as he made sense of the date on the coin. "Am I reading this right?" he marveled. "Is this coin three hundred years old?"

Percy scrutinized the date, sure that Jasper must be mistaken. But it was plain enough; Percy scratched his head. "I don't see how," he said. "It was barely a hundred years ago when the first people got to this island."

"Humph!" Dobro grunted. "A long time before the civilizers showed up, there was plenty of folks on this here island—feechiefolks!"

Aidan pointed at the silver coin. "Does that look like something a feechie would carry around?" he asked. "I've never seen a feechie with a money purse."

"'Course not!" Dobro said with some haughtiness. Even Chief Larbo's band, when under the spell of cold-shiny knives, axes, and shovels, never had any use for cold-shiny money. "I was just makin' a point," Dobro continued. "Just because there ain't no civilizers on a island don't mean there ain't no people."

"I take your point," said Percy, somewhat chastened.

Jasper was still studying the ancient coin. It must have been made from the purest silver, for it was hardly tarnished. The portrait on the front was still easy to make out—a thickset man with an enormous beard and a four-cornered hat or crown on his head. Jasper's finger traced a pair of branching sticks that appeared to sprout from the figure's head. "Are those supposed to be tree limbs behind his head?" he asked. "Is this some kind of forest king?"

Errol took the coin from his son and examined it. "Those aren't tree limbs," he said. "Those are antlers."

"So this is . . ." Jasper began. His lips were parted in astonishment.

Errol nodded. "I think it must be."

All twenty of the men at the diggings looked expectantly from Errol to Jasper and back again, waiting for an explanation. But the father and his studious son both fell silent, brows creased in perplexity.

"This must be what?" asked Percy. "This must be who?"

"King Halverd the Antlered," said Aidan, the light finally dawning on him. "The first king of Halverdy."

Arliss and several of the other Greasy Cave boys looked blank. They were no scholars. "Where's Halverdy?" Arliss asked.

"It's on the continent," said Jasper. "Or used to be. Most of the first people to come to Corenwald . . ."

"Most of the first *civilizers*," Dobro corrected.

"Right. Most of the first *civilizers*," Jasper continued, acknowledging Dobro's correction, "were Halverdens who left the continent when their kingdom finally fell to the Pyrthens in the middle of the last century. Our ancestors were Halverdens. Yours probably were, too, Arliss."

Jasper pointed to the face on the coin his father still held. "Halverdy got its name from this man—Halverd the Antlered. It was he who first united the warring tribes of the continent's eastern plains and great forest into a single kingdom to fight the Pyrthen hordes that were sweeping in from the north and west."

But Arliss was only minimally interested in continental history. He wanted to know more about this Halverd. "But how in the world," he asked, "did he get antlers?"

Jasper laughed. "He probably just attached a pair to his helmet. His crown was decorated with antlers too. But he went down in the old lore as Halverd the Antlered, as if the antlers had sprouted from his head."

"Like Harvo Hornhead," Dobro offered, as if everyone knew exactly what he was talking about.

"Like who?" asked Arliss. Though Arliss famously had the "miner's head" for finding his way underground, he had no head for history. He was already feeling overwhelmed by Jasper's discourse, without adding feechie history to the mix.

"You know, Chief Harvo, the first Feechie chief," said Dobro, a little exasperated at the poor miner's ignorance. "Head like a buck deer, body like a he-feechie." Arliss still looked blank. Dobro continued. "Harvo was the one what caught six turkeys at one time. Put his head down and run through a flock of them. Skewered the rascals on his antlers. Then he roasted them. Just leaned out over the fire with them dangling from his antlers."

Everybody was listening, but to Dobro's chagrin, only Aidan knew what he was talking about. "If you ain't the ignorantest bunch of know-nothings I ever run into!" Dobro exclaimed. "What kind of history do they teach you people?"

Aidan had heard the legends about Chief Harvo while he was living in the Feechiefen. But he had never before considered the similarities between Harvo and Halverd the Antlered.

Errol was holding the coin at arm's length, trying to focus enough to read the inscription on the back. "V-E-Z," he struggled to read. He handed the coin to Brennus. "Your eyes are younger," he said. "What does this say?"

"It's not just your eyes, Father," Brennus said. "This is hard to read. V-E-Z-something-something-something-N-D."

Aidan pointed to a blurred spot in the middle of the inscription. "Is that an L?"

Percy squinted at the coin. "V-E-Z-something-L-something-N-D."

Errol shouted, "Veziland! Veziland! My grandfather used to sing ballads from the old country about Veziland."

"So this coin," began Aidan, speaking slowly because he wanted to be sure he had it right. "This coin came from the place you call Veziland some three hundred years ago—two hundred years before the first civilizers came over from Halverdy."

"Looks that way," Jasper answered.

"But how did it get here?"

"Maybe a coin collector dropped it?" Percy suggested, though not very confidently.

Aidan looked around at the desolate landscape—an inhospitable environment for coin collectors. "Doesn't seem very likely."

"Maybe this is an old feechie settlement," said Brennus. "Maybe feechies traded with Vezilanders three hundred years ago, before any civilizers came over."

Dobro scoffed at the idea. "This ain't no feechie settlement. Feechiefolks don't cut down trees to make cabins." He pointed at the corroded plowshare they had found earlier. "Feechiefolks don't scratch up the ground with cold-shiny blades. And feechiefolks don't live in holes in the ground!"

Dobro had a point. Nothing they had found at this site suggested feechiefolk.

"Maybe we've always had it wrong," said Percy. "Maybe civilizers got here earlier than we thought."

"We haven't been wrong about that," Errol insisted. "All four of my grandparents came in the first flotilla from the continent. I know for a fact that there weren't any civilizers on this island when they got here."

Aidan took the coin in his hand again and wondered if he would ever see through to its puzzling origins.

‡ ‡ ‡

After morning drills a few days later, Errol took Aidan aside. "I think it's time you went to see this Lynwood," he said. "The chief of the Aidanites. The chair of the—what was it?—the Secret Committee for the Ascendancy of the Wilderking?"

"I thought he might come see us," Aidan said.

"From what I know of Lynwood," said Errol, "he's not the sort to go to that much trouble if there's someone he can pay or cajole to do it for him."

"Who is he?"

"He's a merchant and a very wealthy one. Lives with his wife and daughters in one of the finest houses in Tambluff."

"If he's so rich, what does he want with a new king? Sounds like things have gone well enough under the old king."

Errol thought on the question. "I don't really know the man; we met only once or twice, so most of what I know of him is second hand. But he strikes me as the kind of man who wants to have a king who owes him a favor. He's done well enough under King Darrow, but Darrow doesn't know him from Adam. He'd risk a charge of treason for the satisfaction of being in a king's inner circle."

"Is he a bad man?" Aidan asked.

"He's a man who doesn't know his own heart. He probably tells himself he does everything for the good of Corenwald, and he probably believes it.

"Now that he's given you an army, it's probably only fair that you should tell him where you stand with things." Errol thought for a moment, then his eyes brightened with an idea. "Dobro's been dying to get out of these canyons."

"Time to leave these neighborhoods," said Aidan.

"Right. If anything would throw cold water on Lynwood's desire for a Wilderking, it might be having a genuine feechie in his house. Why don't you take Dobro along?"

Chapter Sixteen

Ma Pearl's Public House

The village of Ryelan was the nearest civilization to Sinking Canyons, ten leagues across scrubby plain. In truth, it just barely counted as civilization. The mean little village was the sort of place people left the first chance they got. But horses could be bought there, so Aidan and Dobro made it their first stop on their journey to Tambluff. They wore hooded robes over their tunics to conceal their identities.

"Listen here, Dobro," Aidan said when the low buildings of the village came into view. "I think it's going to be better if you don't talk while we're in Ryelan. We need to draw as little attention to ourselves as possible. And if we can keep people from noticing you're a feechie, so much the better."

"Seems a shame," said Dobro, who had begun to think of himself as something of a feechie ambassador to the civilizers.

"Here's the thing," said Aidan. "Even if you don't mind breaking the Feechie Code—"

"Aw, Aidan," Dobro interrupted, "half the civilizers in Corenwald believes in feechies these days."

"That's not the point," Aidan insisted. "When people realize who you are, they realize who I am. You heard what those militiamen were saying. Everybody's been talking about how I brought a feechie with me when I came out of the Feechiefen."

"Folks don't say you come with one feechie," Dobro corrected. "They say you come with a whole mess of feechies." He took some pride in the fact that popular gossip had multiplied him into a band of feechie warriors.

"The last thing we need is a bunch of Aidanites and Wilderkingers following us to Tambluff. So when we get to Ryelan, don't speak to anybody." He thought about Dobro's green teeth; tooth brushing was one aspect of civilizer life Dobro hadn't yet mastered. "Don't smile at anybody either."

"What if I see a pretty civilizer lady?" Dobro asked.

"If you see a pretty civilizer lady, believe me, she doesn't want to see your teeth. And whatever you do, don't breathe on anyone."

‡ ‡ ‡

There was more activity than Aidan had expected in the little village. The dust from the main street lay in a thick cloud, kicked up by people going back and forth. The activity seemed to center on the general store. Only it wasn't called a general store anymore. On the façade above the entrance, a new sign had been nailed over the old one. It read "Sinking Canyon Outfitters. One stop for all your camping and militia-related needs." A string of wagons stretched along the front of the store, waiting there to unload their supplies of boots, ropes, water bladders, hardtack biscuit, dried beef, swords, shovels—everything a militiaman might need to make Sinking Canyons more livable.

Aidan hurried past the scene on his way to a public house called Ma Pearl's two doors down. "It's almost noon," he said to Dobro. "Let's get some dinner here and save the food in our packs. I'm sure somebody here can direct me to a horse trader."

The little dining room was nearly full and loud with the raucous conversation and laughter of the rough locals. All eyes followed Aidan and Dobro as they pushed their way to an empty table in the back.

After they were seated, a rough voice from two tables away called in their direction. "You boys hiked in from the south, didn't you?"

Aidan nodded his head.

"Sinking Canyons?" the man asked.

Aidan craned his neck to see if the innkeeper were coming.

"'Course Sinking Canyons, you half-wit," shouted a walleyed man at another table. "Coming from the south. Where else would they be coming from?"

"Must be a couple of Aidanites," another man observed. "Say, when you boys figure to march on Tambluff Castle?"

The walleyed man snorted. "They better march on

it soon if they don't want to find Pyrthens when they get there!"

"Don't matter to me who lives in Tambluff Castle," the first man declared. "Long as they leave me alone, I mean to leave them alone. Tambluff's a long way from Ryelan."

"Say," said the walleyed man, directing his attention back to Aidan and Dobro, "I reckon you boys has seen this Aidan Errolson?"

Aidan and Dobro looked down at the table, trying to pretend they hadn't heard the man.

"I'm talking to you boys," the man repeated a little more loudly, refusing to be ignored. "I asked if you boys has seen Aidan Errolson."

"You know, the Wilderking," said another.

"Watch for the Wilderking!" boomed another with false portentousness.

"Yes, we've seen him," Aidan finally answered, hoping to avoid trouble.

"I wouldn't mind getting a look at that feller," said the walleyed man, getting a look at the feller even as he said it. "I hear he goes around with a whole gang of mean-looking feechies. Is that true?"

Dobro drew his hand over his mouth, trying to stifle a smile of pleasure at his inflated reputation.

"No," Aidan answered. "It's just one feechie, a scrawny rat of a fellow, acts like he doesn't have good sense half the time."

A man in the far corner shouted across the room, "If you Aidanites think a Wilderking is any different from a

King Darrow or a Pyrthen king—or a feechie king, for that matter—then you Aidanites is a pack of fools."

His opinion was met with hoots of agreement and support from across the crowded room.

Ma Pearl, the innkeeper, finally arrived at the table. She was a stout, jolly-faced woman, and she wiped her hands on her apron as she said, "Fools or no, them Aidanites has sure been good for business. You want lunch, sugar?"

Aidan and Dobro both nodded their heads.

"I got bacon, collard greens, and sweet potatoes."

"Bring us two," Aidan said. "And some water if you don't mind. And could you tell me where I could find a horse trader?"

Ma Pearl directed him to a stable on the other side of the dusty street, and Aidan, eager to keep their visit to Ryelan as short as possible, left Dobro waiting at the table while he went out to buy their horses.

"Remember," he whispered in Dobro's ear before he left, "no talking. No fighting. No grinning."

It wasn't long at all before Ma Pearl brought the plates to Dobro's table. And Dobro, figuring that Aidan probably wouldn't want him to wait, dug in. Like tooth brushing, eating with utensils was one of those civilizer niceties Dobro hadn't yet embraced. He had just shoved a fistful of collard greens into his mouth when a big farmhand sat down across from him in Aidan's chair. "Say, stranger," he said, "where you come from anyway?"

Remembering what Aidan had said, Dobro just

looked blankly at the man. He didn't speak. He didn't smile. A drop of green pot liquor dripped from his chin and back onto the pile of collard greens from which it had come.

"What's a matter with you, boy?" the big Ryelanite asked. "Cat got your tongue?"

"Get after him, Lumley," one of the diners urged.

"Come on, Lum," yelled another.

Dobro just shrugged and thumbed a glob of sweet potato into his mouth.

"You stuck up or what?" Lumley leaned across the table and put his face just inches from Dobro's. Dobro remembered Aidan's warning about breathing on the locals, so he put up a hand to shield his mouth and nose.

"Oh, so my breath stinks, does it?" Lumley was yelling now, and everybody in the place was watching intently to see what would happen next.

"Well, stranger," Lumley continued, "I 'bout had it with outsiders coming here and looking down their noses at us Ryelan folks."

Dobro looked down at his plate. There was no stopping the big field hand now. "I may not be from Tambluff or Middenmarsh or whatever fancy place you come from, stranger, but I mean for you to know that Ryelanites is as good as anybody. You gonna howdy me and be neighborly, or I'm gonna find out why."

Lumley was off his chair now, looming over Dobro with a fist drawn back. "Am I gonna have to learn you manners the hard way?"

Dobro's shrug and close-lipped little smile was more than Lumley could tolerate. He roared like a bear as his left fist rocketed toward Dobro's right ear. But Dobro was much quicker than any big field hand's fist. He easily ducked under it, and Lumley's knuckles cracked against the timber that held up the roof above them. He screamed with pain and lunged at Dobro with a sweeping right. Dobro dodged that, too, and Lumley's momentum sent the table crashing to the ground.

Dobro leaped onto the nearest table and headed for the door, dodging from tabletop to tabletop as the diners dove for him and grabbed at his ankles. Food, crockery, forks, and knives tumbled to the floor with a crash and a clatter. Tables tipped, and people slipped on the smashed sweet potatoes and greasy collard greens that littered the floor.

When Dobro reached the door, he found it to be guarded by three very large Ryelanites. Dobro felt confident he could whip them, but he had orders not to fight, so he jumped from a tabletop to one of the exposed rafters above. He pulled himself up and ran from rafter to rafter, dodging broken plates and mugs the diners were hurling at him.

By this time, Ma Pearl had waded into the fray, swinging her black iron skillet like a battle ax, trying to subdue the rowdies who were tearing her public house apart. Big men fell like mown wheat under Pearl's skillet; their thick heads rang like gongs.

Dobro, meanwhile, found a way out onto the

thatched roof. Aidan was coming around from the stable leading two horses. His face was a mask of horror when he heard the uproar coming from Ma Pearl's inn. The very walls were shaking.

"Aidan!" Dobro shouted. "Time to leave these neighborhoods!" Aidan led the horses across to the eave where Dobro was waiting for him. Dobro dropped onto the horse's haunches, and they took off at a mad gallop as angry Ryelanites came boiling out the front door of Ma Pearl's.

Aidan rode easy in the saddle as his horse weaved through the villagers who came into the street to see what the ruckus was. His horsemanship returned naturally after so many years. Dobro, on the other hand, rode standing up like a circus rider. As the village receded in the distance, he waved his thanks to Ma Pearl, who was still brandishing her black skillet.

"I told you not to get into any fights," Aidan yelled when they were out of immediate danger.

"I wasn't fighting," Dobro said. "I was just running away from the fight. But that only seemed to make them more angrified."

"What did you say to those people?" Aidan asked hotly.

"I didn't say a word the whole time I was there," Dobro insisted. Then he confessed, "But, Aidan, when them old boys was chasin' me acrost the tabletops, I did grin a little bit. I just couldn't help it."

Chapter Seventeen

South Gate

idan still knew the River Road bend for bend. "Over this next rise," he called to Dobro behind him, "we'll get our first glimpse of Tambluff Castle." He turned around in the saddle to look at his feechie friend. "Dobro!" he shouted, exasperation in his voice. "You have to sit down in the saddle. I mean it!" Dobro had ridden most of the way from Ryelan, standing up on his horse's back.

"I can see more this way," Dobro said.

"We're trying *not* to draw attention to ourselves," Aidan said.

"Ain't that what these hoods is for? To keep folks from recognizin' us?"

"Yes, Dobro, but if you're carrying on like a trick rider . . ."

"It just don't seem right to me, settin' on a critter's back," said Dobro. "Don't seem respectful to the critter."

"Dobro, sit down!"

Dobro flopped into his horse's saddle, slumping like a petulant child. "Yes, Your Majesty," he said. Sarcasm was one of the civilizer habits he was starting to get the hang of.

"In an hour we're going to be in Tambluff," Aidan said. "It's not like any place you've ever seen before. Busy streets, fine carriages. Guards everywhere. Soldiers. People whose job is to pay attention to who comes in and who goes out. If you don't try a little harder to blend in with the civilizers, we're going to be in a whole world of trouble, Dobro."

"I'll try harder, Aidan," said Dobro. "But you folks is got such peculiar ways, it ain't easy to blend in."

"Just try to do what everybody else is doing."

They approached the city at the south gate and merged with the steady flow of people threading under the teeth of the portcullis. Dobro pulled his hood further over his face, suddenly self-conscious among so many civilizers, aware of how different he was from them.

Before they reached the gate, the door to the gate-house swung open, and a round old man leaped in front of them holding a pikestaff across his body to block their way. "You!" he shouted. "You hooded horsemen. You'll identify yourselves before you pass through my gate."

The old man was Southporter, keeper of this gate since well before Aidan was born. How many times had Southporter welcomed Aidan to Tambluff when he was younger? King Darrow never had a more faithful servant. Perhaps he would not look so kindly on Aidan anymore. The armed guards at the gate looked alert, watching the confrontation, ready to get involved if need be.

Aidan had no choice but to identify himself and pray for the best. He could run if he had to; he knew every nook and cranny of Tambluff. And he had no cause to fear on Dobro's account. The wily feechie could take care of himself. Aidan leaned down toward Southporter so the old gatekeeper could see his face under the hood. "I am Aidan Errolson," he whispered.

Southporter's face paled, and he staggered back a step. "Aidan," he whispered. Then, after a quick glance at the armed guards, he opened his arms in a gesture of welcome to Aidan and Dobro. "Simon!" he said heartily. "Thurston! What took you so long? Come in! Come in!"

He turned back to the gate guards. "Can you keep an eye on things until I get my friends settled? It will only take a minute." He herded Aidan and Dobro into the gatehouse and sat them down on a bench he used for questioning suspicious strangers (and sometimes used for taking afternoon naps).

"Aidan, what are you doing in Tambluff?" he whispered, his voice full of genuine concern. "This is the most dangerous place you could possibly be!"

"I've come to—" Aidan began, but Southporter was at it again.

"And who is this with you?" Southporter threw back Dobro's hood and squinted at him, trying to remember if he had ever seen him, or even anybody like him, before.

"Southporter, this is Dobro Turtlebane," Aidan began.

Southporter nodded his head and pointed at Dobro. "I know what you are," he said. "Yes." He kept looking at Dobro, kept nodding. Then he looked back at Aidan. "So it's true. I thought it was just another wild rumor, you traipsing around the countryside with a feechie, but here he is, setting right here in my gatehouse." He stared another moment at Dobro. "He *is* a feechie, ain't he?"

Aidan nodded.

"You've brung some astonishing things to this gatehouse," Southporter said. "Six years ago, you brung the biggest alligator I ever seen before or since. And today, you have brung a feechie in the flesh." He slapped his thighs. "I don't know how you gonna top this one, Aidan!"

Dobro gave Southporter a greenish grin. Southporter shook his head in amazement. Then he grew suddenly serious. "Aidan, there's another rumor about you, and every time I hear it I tell folks it's a filthy lie." He lowered his voice to a whisper. "Folks say you and your pap's training a rebel army down in Sinking Canyons. And I tell them, 'That's a filthy lie, and I don't care who knows it! Ain't nobody,' I tell them, 'ain't nobody truer to the House of Darrow than Lord Errol and his boys.' I still call him 'lord,' even if King Darrow don't. And I tell them, 'Anybody cares to contradict me can have my pikestaff right across his skull bone.'"

Southporter had plenty more to say on that subject, and he meant to go on at some length, but he noticed a strange expression on Aidan's face. Southporter tried to soldier on. "It's like I tell them . . ." He broke off. "Aidan, why ain't you looking at my eyes? Aidan? Oh, dear me, no! Aidan? You *are* training a army in Sinking Canyons!"

"Southporter, it's not what you think!"

Southporter's face crumpled and tears stood in his eyes. "Traitor?" His tone of voice was half-way between an accusation and a question. "Aidan Errolson a traitor?" He put his hand on the bell pull that would summon the armed guards.

"No! Never!" Aidan looked into Southporter's eyes, resisting the temptation to look at his hand on the bell pull. "Believe me, Southporter. Errol and his sons are no traitors. Yes, we are training an army, an army to place at the service of the House of Darrow. These men insist on following me, Southporter. I will lead them in service to Corenwald."

Southporter was silent for a moment. He looked at his hand on the bell pull, then back at Aidan. "Why should I believe you?"

Aidan blinked slowly and said, "Do you even have to ask that?"

Southporter took his hand off the bell pull. He looked a little ashamed of himself. He also looked relieved. "No, Aidan, of course I don't. But you have to admit it looks suspicious. The king outlaws a nobleman and his sons. The nobleman and his sons train an army of malcontents."

"Father says we may be the only army Corenwald has."

Southporter nodded his head. "He may be right. Darrow's army was in terrible shape even before he tried to invade the Feechiefen. Since then, it's been even worse. When the Pyrthens come . . ." Southporter broke off. He shook all over, as if from a sudden chill.

"So you think the Pyrthens are coming too?"

"How could they not be? The question isn't *if* they'll come; it's *when.* And why they haven't already is a mystery to me. I figured the two of you were Pyrthen spies or assassins when you rode up hooded. What are you doing in Tambluff anyway?"

"Seeing the sights," said Dobro with admirable candor. "I ain't never been to the city before, and I made Aidan bring me."

"And I'm here," Aidan began, "to meet with Lynwood Wertenson."

A flicker of suspicion returned to Southporter's eyes. "The rabble-rouser?"

Aidan raised an eyebrow.

"I got no use for that man," said Southporter, "and I don't care who knows it. What business do you have with him?"

"I've come to tell him that I don't intend to lead his rebellion, Southporter."

"That's my boy," whooped Southporter. "That's my boy!"

Aidan wrote a quick note to Lynwood expressing his wish to see the Chair of the Committee at his earliest convenience. Southporter sent the note with his most trusted messenger, then settled in to give Aidan the news from Tambluff. He said he hadn't seen King Darrow since the day he galloped home from Last Camp, after the aborted invasion of the Feechiefen.

"He come thundering through my gate on that beautiful black horse of his," Southporter said, "face like a wild man." He turned to Dobro. "No offense intended, of course."

The wild man nodded and smiled greenly. "None taken."

"Galloping so hard his mounted bodyguard couldn't keep up with him. Galloped into the castle, and so far as anybody knows, he ain't come out since. Hasn't met with the Four and Twenty Nobles, hasn't seen anybody besides his personal servants and Prince Steren.

"The servants say he raves and rages for whole days at a time. Goes back and forth between wanting to pardon you and wanting to hunt you down and kill you. So he ends up not doing anything." Southporter shook his head. "I think your act of mercy—choosing not to kill him when you had the chance—got inside his mind and busted it up. He's been hating so long he can't make sense out of mercy. Sounds like he can't make sense of nothing else either. He done the same thing in the days after you brought home the frog orchid. Tore up with guilt for hating a feller who always answers good for bad, but still hating you all the more for it."

Aidan's heart went out to his friend the prince. "What about Steren?" he asked. "What has he been doing?"

"He's been away for three weeks. His father sent him out looking for you."

Aidan thought on this. "It wouldn't take three weeks to hunt me down. Doesn't everybody in Corenwald know we're in Sinking Canyons?"

Southporter laughed. "The children playing in the street out there know you're in Sinking Canyons. Of course, they also think you're in Sinking Canyons with an army of ten thousand feechiefolk, all foaming at the mouth and ready to tear down Tambluff brick by brick."

Dobro managed to stifle a little smile, but he did sit up a little straighter.

"So Steren must not be trying very hard to find me," said Aidan.

"Doesn't sound like it," said Southporter. "Sounds like he's protecting his old friend. Or maybe," he added after a brief reflection, "he's afraid of what he might find if he does track you down."

"When Steren comes back, Southporter, would you make sure he knows what I told you? That army in Sinking Canyons is his army—Corenwald's army—not mine."

Southporter smiled. "I'll make sure he knows."

By that time the messenger was back with Lynwood's reply. He requested the honor of Aidan's and Dobro's presence at his supper table that evening. The supper hour was fast approaching, so Southporter loaded Aidan and Dobro into his pony cart and covered them with a blanket. It wouldn't do for Southporter to be seen with these hooded strangers. Nor would it do for him to be seen at Lynwood's house. So when he reached the street corner where Lynwood's house stood, he stopped for a passing wagon and made a low whistle. Aidan and Dobro tumbled out the back of the cart, and Southporter rolled on without a backward look or a wave.

Chapter Eighteen

Lynwood's House

Try to blend in," Aidan whispered as they mounted the marble steps to Lynwood's house. Somehow he knew Dobro wouldn't blend in. They were in the finest neighborhood in all of Tambluff. A gleaming carriage rattled by, pulled by a horse whose carefully groomed flanks shone in the afternoon sun. Lynwood's massive front door was polished walnut. The brass of its great alligator-head knocker was so bright Aidan hated to touch it at all.

"Everything's so shiny!" Dobro marveled.

The servant who answered Lynwood's door was dressed as finely as a Pyrthen lord, in tailored silks and white hose and gold buckles on his shoes. Dobro whistled when he saw him and nudged Aidan. "Even the folks is shiny!"

The man hurried the two dusty travelers into the entry hall, peering out into the street to see if anyone had noticed them. "Follow me ... gentlemen," he said. There was that tiny pause, barely perceptible, before he said the word *gentlemen.* Ebbe used to do the same thing when ushering people he considered to be beneath the dignity of Errol's house. Dobro, of course, didn't notice.

The servant led them through wide arches, past great banks of windows, substantial fireplaces, gracefully appointed furniture, huge portraits in heavy frames, a suit of armor standing in a corner. Finely dressed servants swished through, turning around to stare at the strangers after they had passed.

"What's your name?" Dobro asked the back of the servant.

The servant made not quite a quarter turn in Dobro's direction without slacking his pace. "I'm the butler," he said in a tone meant to convey that in his line of work he didn't ask personal questions and shouldn't be expected to answer any.

"Butler," said Dobro. "That's a nice name. I'm Dobro, and this here's Aidan."

The butler didn't react to Dobro's introductions. He opened a pair of very tall, narrow doors and gestured Aidan and Dobro into a high-ceilinged, airy room. A bearded man, probably in his fifties, his wife, and four beautiful young women, their daughters, all rose from richly embroidered chairs. Lynwood directed the butler from the room with an elegant nod, and when the servant had glided noiselessly away, he beamed an ingratiating smile at Aidan and bowed deeply. "Aidan Errolson," he said, "I am honored to have you in my home."

Aidan popped a quick bow, but his social graces were still rusty. "We are pleased to be here," Aidan said, not altogether convincingly. In the Feechiefen and in Sinking Canyons, he had abandoned the habit of saying things he didn't mean. "This is my very good friend Dobro Turtlebane." Lynwood and his family, turning their attention to Dobro for the first time, all opened their eyes a little wider, realizing at once that the rumors of Aidan consorting with feechies were surely true. But they managed to maintain their composure.

Dobro gave a closed-lipped little smile. He remembered what Aidan had said about civilizer ladies not wanting to see his teeth. He tipped over in a bow that was even less graceful than Aidan's. Dobro was truly awestruck in the presence of these five women—the mother no less than the daughters. The grandeur of the house had made but little impression on him. But these civilizer ladies—Dobro had no idea such exquisite creatures even existed.

"My wife, Lenora," Dobro could hear Lynwood saying through a buzzing in his ears. "Daughters Onie, Lilla, Jewell, and Sadie."

Their curling hair was swept into carefully arranged piles high atop their heads. Except for the youngest daughter—Sadie, was it? Her hair had already begun to unpile in several unruly tendrils down her neck and in front of her face. Such faces . . . the mother and three of the daughters were as white as boar tusks, as if they had never seen the sunshine. But that youngest girl—yes, it was Sadie—her face was brown, or pink, really, especially on the end of her nose and on her cheeks. She looked as if she had soaked up the sun and was now shining it back on everyone who looked at her. No wonder these girls preferred not to cover their faces in swamp mud! And their arms were as long and thin and graceful as a craney-crow's neck.

Except for Sadie, who seemed to divide her attention equally between the two visitors, the women were all gazing at Aidan with undisguised admiration. Lynwood said something about an honor and a privilege. Whatever he was saying, Dobro couldn't make any sense of it. He felt this same way at the Battle of Bearhouse, after he had been conked on the head. He could see that talking was happening; he could even hear most of the words, but he couldn't make them make sense. He was that taken with the four Lynwood daughters. Then Sadie stuck her tongue out at him, and it brought him back around like a splash of water in the face.

"Retire to the dining room," Lynwood was saying, as he shepherded the group across the hall toward the dining room. Elaborately carved chairs surrounded a table set with blown-glass tumblers and six or seven pieces of silver per place setting.

Lynwood put Aidan near the head of the table, in the place of honor beside his own right hand. Dobro got the second spot of honor, the foot of the table directly across from Lynwood, which meant he was surrounded by Lynwood's daughters, much to the young ladies' disappointment.

While the servants brought out the first course,

a soup of river perch, Lenora got the conversation started with small talk. How was Aidan and Dobro's trip? Wasn't this weather unusual for August? How long did they plan to stay in Tambluff? Aidan answered each question politely but with as little elaboration as possible.

Dobro, meanwhile, was working on his soup, and working rather hard. He held his spoon handle in his fist as if it were the haft of a spear and jabbed it beneath the pieces of fish that bobbed in his fine, white-clay bowl. Then he brought the spoon to his mouth, palm up, slurped the soup loudly, and smacked with satisfaction before plunging the spoon in for another go at it. The small talk around the table stopped as Lynwood and his family stared in horror and confusion at this most outlandish dinner guest. Enraptured by the soup, Dobro didn't notice he had become the center of the room's attention.

Sadie was the first person to speak. She leaned back in her chair, the better to take in the wild and smelly young man in the chair beside her, and she said to Dobro what her parents and sisters were saying silently: "Are you some kind of feechie or something?"

Dobro jerked his head back, amazed at the girl's perceptiveness. "Well, ain't you the clever one?" he said with an admiring smile. "There ain't no hiding the truth from you, is there?" He was quickly mastering his shyness. "I like that in a gal." He winked at Sadie. She blushed and looked down at her soup, twirling a ringlet around a finger.

"I can't lie to a pretty civilizer gal like you," Dobro said. "That would go against the Feechie Code. I *am* a feechie, but my dress and manners done got so refined, most folks take me for a civilizer." He arched the left half of his one long eyebrow and graced the room with a look meant to convey great sophistication. The effect, such as it was, was ruined by a sneeze that came on him as suddenly as a sparrow hawk. He was not accustomed to the ground black pepper served at civilizer tables.

Dobro grabbed the corner of the tablecloth and blew his nose into it with a great trumpeting. He gave Sadie a broad wink. "Like that right there. Time was, I'd a wiped my nose on the back of my hand." He pantomimed raking his nose from his knuckles nearly to his elbow. "But now I takened to blowing it in a cloth, just like a civilizer."

Dobro mistook the shocked silence for rapt attention, and it emboldened him to keep talking. "It's the little things makes a feller blend in, ain't it?" He slurped up another spoonful of soup. "And if there's one thing a feechie knows about, it's blending in. I remember one time I was cooling off in a seep hole, and I was blended in so good a alligator nearbout stepped on me." His bashfulness was completely gone by now. A little bashfulness would have done him some good.

"This here alligator just noozled up beside of me. I was so blended in, you see, that he thought he was by his lonesome. I raised up and *frammed* him in the snout." With that he put his two fists together like a club and crashed them down on the table, causing plates, bowls, silver, and blown-glass tumblers to leap an inch off the planks of the tabletop. A roll tumbled off the table and circled around Aidan's feet.

The crash and the reproachful looks from the ladies were enough to abash Dobro at last. His face pinkened with embarrassment, and he returned his full attention to his soup. He didn't even notice the look of admiration that beamed from Sadie's face.

Lynwood thought it best to get down to business before Dobro got started again. He turned toward his wife. "The hope of Corenwald, seated at our very table, Lenora. Can you believe it?"

Lenora beamed a charming smile at Aidan. "We so longed for your return from the Feechiefen, Aidan, for the fulfillment of the prophecy. We were beside ourselves with joy when we heard you were back on this side of the river."

"I hope you will forgive my eagerness to move things along, Aidan," said Lynwood, "what with the local committees and the Aidanite militias and the posters on the trees. We figure there's no point putting off the inevitable—no, the foreordained—is there?"

"That's actually what I came to speak with you about," Aidan began, but Lynwood cut him off.

"Three thousand men at your disposal, Aidan. What does that kind of power feel like?"

"Now wait a minute," Aidan tried to interrupt. But Lynwood pressed on.

"I love to give good gifts—as my darling Lenora and my daughters can attest." Lenora and the girls eagerly nodded their heads, except Sadie, who blew a stray wisp of hair out of her eyes. "And I had been waiting years to give that gift to the Wilderking: a whole army of loyal men willing to fight to the death for you against"—he reined himself in—"against tyranny." He grinned a sly, knowing grin. "So what do you say our next steps are, Aidan?" At last he paused to give Aidan a chance to speak.

Aidan's eyes narrowed as he prepared to speak. "I did not come here to scheme with you," he said firmly but quietly. "I want no part of your conspiracy against the anointed king." A look of confusion overspread Lynwood's face. Aidan pressed on. "You have sent me an army, and I thank you for it. I will lead them. But I won't lead them against King Darrow."

Lynwood's brow was knitted with perplexity. He had prepared for many, many possibilities but never this one. It had never occurred to him the Wilderking might not welcome his efforts on his behalf. "Not lead our army against King Darrow?" he said. "Why do you think I gave them to you?"

"I know full well why you 'gave them' to me, Lynwood," Aidan answered. "But I won't shed Corenwalder blood for the sake of my ambition—or for the sake of yours."

Leonora broke in. "But, Aidan, surely you know yourself to be the Wilderking of ancient prophecy. What about the panther you slew with a stone? What about the Pyrthen giant? What about the feechiefolk? You have to believe you're the Wilderking." She paused, her confidence slipping. "Don't you believe it?"

"I believe the living God raises kings and brings them down," Aidan answered. "I believe we don't have to force ourselves on the ancient prophecies. I believe a traitor is no fit king." He turned his gaze to Lynwood. "If you want to follow me, Lynwood, then follow me. But don't try to lead me like a bull with a nose ring, and all the while pretend you're following me."

Lynwood looked down at his knuckles, the expression on his face shifting from disappointment to embarrassment to something more like anger. Another awkward silence descended on the room. It was broken this time by loud sucking noises at the far end of the table, where Dobro was picking his teeth with his fork.

Lynwood exploded in an outburst of irritability. "Could someone do something with that infernal heathen?" He pointed at Dobro with all five fingers. "Could you at least have the decency to act like a human being at my table?"

"Lynwood, don't you understand?" said Aidan. "When the Wilderking comes, he won't be coming to bring you more of this." He gestured around at the finery of Lynwood's house. "He's probably going to bring you a little more of that." He pointed at Dobro, who was moping after Lynwood's rebuke.

Lenora gasped—squeaked, really.

"Think about it," Aidan continued. "'Leading his troops of wild men and brutes.' Are you sure that's what you want? A bunch of wild feechies running loose in Corenwald? That's what the Wilderking will bring with him. Feechies free to leave their forest haunts and live among the rest of us, if that's what they want to do."

Aidan chuckled. "If you're backing me for king, you need to know that's what you're backing."

Lynwood grew pale behind his beard. Lenora was fanning herself with quick, choppy strokes. And three of the sisters' faces were contorted into expressions of undisguised contempt for the feechie at their table. But Sadie's eyes twinkled at the prospect of feechie-folk in Tambluff.

From the hallway came the sound of a mailed fist pounding on the front door. A gruff and threatening voice penetrated the thick walnut. "Open up! In the name of King Darrow, open up!"

Chapter Nineteen

The Ferry Keeper's Daughter

veryone froze, like statues arranged around a dinner table. "Spies," Lynwood hissed. "King Darrow has spies in the neighborhood. They must have seen you come in."

The first person to act was Sadie. She grabbed Dobro by the hand and, motioning for Aidan to follow, ran out of the dining room and down the corridor, away from the entry hall. They dashed through the rambling house and out a back door opening onto an alleyway. It was dark already, and they were able to get to the street without being detected. But just barely. Armed men in the blue uniforms of King Darrow's castle guard seemed to be everywhere.

Following Sadie's example, Aidan and Dobro didn't run but walked as calmly as they could manage. Any second, though, one of these guards was going to realize who they were. Or perhaps the guards would just start arresting everybody on the street.

When they turned another corner, they saw a great crowd of people congregated on the sidewalk. Aidan's first impulse was to run, to seek seclusion. But Sadie, the city girl, knew there was no better place to hide than in a crowd. She led Aidan and Dobro straight into the throng. Then Aidan realized what had drawn the crowd. They were standing outside the Swan Theater where, according to the sign above, *The Ferry Keeper's Daughter* was playing.

Sadie walked boldly up to the ticket seller's booth and bought three tickets for the balcony.

It was dark in the theater. There was little chance of anyone recognizing them here. Aidan could see from Sadie's silhouette that her hair had given up all efforts at respectability. Some of it hung in limp curls, and some jutted out at odd angles, like the hair of a she-feechie. Dobro thought she was beautiful.

When they were settled in their seats, thirty feet above the stage, Sadie lost all composure and folded herself over in her seat. Her face was covered in cupped hands, and her shoulders were shaking.

Aidan and Dobro, seated on either side of her, stared at one another. They had handled plenty of sticky situations together, but neither of them knew what to do about a crying woman. Sadie had reason enough to cry, poor thing. Her whole family no doubt was in the clutches of King Darrow's men. What's more, her father was guilty as charged. Dobro raised a hand to pat her on the back, but when she raised herself up, they realized it was giggling, not sobbing, that shook her frame.

"Have you ... ever had ... this much fun?" she whispered between fits of laughter. "Supper with a feechie ... escape from the castle guard ... now a play!" A nearby patron of the theater shushed her, but Sadie couldn't help herself.

"But what about your family?" Aidan whispered. "Aren't you worried about them?"

"Not at all," she whispered back. "Not at all. Papa's been ready for this for years. He dug a tunnel. Everybody pops down the tunnel. They pop back up in one of our other houses. Perfect escape. No, don't worry about them."

When the orchestra struck up, Dobro jumped a foot off his seat and clutched his ears. He liked music well enough, but he had never seen more than a pipe and drum at a feechiesing, or the occasional fiddle by the campfire at Sinking Canyons. The sound of a whole orchestra in an enclosed place was overwhelming. "Where is that racket comin' from?" he demanded.

"Down there." Aidan pointed to a spot in front of the stage. "In the pit."

Dobro peered over the balcony railing and saw, just below the dimmed foot lanterns, the violinists sawing away, the trumpeters blowing for all they were worth, a xylophonist running up for the high notes and down for the low notes, and a drummer pounding at a big bass drum.

"Whoever flung them folks in the pit had the right idea," Dobro judged, "but it don't seem to have slowed them down none."

A woman in a neighboring seat shushed him, but Dobro, who had never been shushed before, thought she had sneezed and kept talking at the same volume. "What is all these folks setting here in the dark for?" he asked. "Who they hiding from, you reckon?"

"They're not hiding," Aidan whispered. "This is an entertainment."

"Like a feechiesing?"

"Sort of. But not exactly. It's a play."

"Play?" Dobro looked around the darkened theater. "I don't see what game this many folks could play. If they all took turns at a gator grabble, the poor gator'd be slap wore out before they got halfway through. And these folks ain't dressed for fistfights."

"No, they're not here *to* play," Aidan whispered back. "They're here to *see* a play." He couldn't figure out how to explain a play to Dobro. The feechies did a lot of storytelling, but they didn't do drama or playacting. As it turned out, however, he didn't have a chance to explain. The foot lanterns were brightened, the curtain rose, and the play explained itself.

The scene was a ferry landing, complete with cut-out trees standing in front of a painted backdrop of a muddy river. Dobro was spellbound. "How they get trees to grow inside a building?" he wondered aloud.

The lead character, the ferry keeper's daughter, was played by a fresh-faced girl in a peasant dress. She paced up and down the front of the stage and fetched a long sigh before launching into a soliloquy.

"That's gal's a loud talker!" Dobro observed. "I can hear her all the way up here!"

"Not half as loud as you!" hissed a theatergoer behind him.

The ferry keeper's daughter poured out her troubles in that opening speech. Her father had been too sick to operate the ferry, so he had missed two months of payments to the moneylender. Now the moneylender wanted a bag of gold before midnight, or he would take away the ferry keeper's house, leaving the old man and his faithful daughter with nowhere to go.

Dobro was struck to the heart. He leaned across Sadie to whisper in Aidan's ear. "Did you hear that gal? We got to help her." He snatched Aidan's side pouch and started digging around in it. "You still got that bag of gold you had when you bought them horses?"

Aidan grabbed his side pouch back. "Dobro, it's just a play. She's just acting. She's not really in trouble."

The actress was stretched out on the floor, convulsed with sobs. Dobro started crying too. "Look at her!" he said through his tears. "You gonna sit there and tell me that gal's troubles ain't real?" The look he gave Aidan dripped with disappointment and reproach. "Your heart is as cold as a cottonmouth, Aidan Errolson, and as black as a squirrel's eye."

The theater erupted with boos and hisses when the villain strode across the stage. The moneylender was a tall man in a black cape and a black hat, with black, curling mustaches. He stood over the crumpled, shuddering form of the ferry keeper's daughter, his hands on his hips, his feet spread wide. He told the beautiful girl he would cancel her father's debt if only she would marry him. She spat on the ground where he stood. Dobro loved her for it.

The ferry keeper's daughter turned to run, but the villain caught her by the shoulders and turned her roughly around to face him.

For Dobro, that was the last straw. "I've seen enough of this!" he shrieked as he jumped onto the back of his chair. "Come on, boys, let's get him!"

"Dobro, sit down," Aidan ordered in a loud whisper.

"I ain't settin' down until after that moneylender's whupped," Dobro declared. "I don't aim to watch that feller insult and abuse a sufferin' innocent another minute." He raised a fist in the air. "Who's with me?"

To Dobro's astonishment, nobody was with him. Everybody in the whole place seemed content to sit and watch the moneylender insult and abuse the poor ferry keeper's daughter.

The play had come to a halt by now. The actors had stopped acting and were staring up into the darkness, trying to see what the commotion was. The musicians in the pit had stood up, too, and were peering toward the nasally voice shrilling thirty feet above their heads.

When Aidan realized what Dobro was about to do, he lunged to stop him. But he was a split second too late. Dobro jumped from the balcony and made a high, beautiful arc out over the patrons in the lower-level seats. At the top of his leap, he grabbed a thick curtain rope that looped down from the ceiling. He hurtled down toward the stage in a great swoop. "Haaa-wwwweeeeee!" he yodeled, as he let go of the rope and landed on all fours in front of the money-lender. The black-clad blackguard tried to run, but Dobro caught him by the cape and flung him to the floor. Then he rolled him, wrapping the cape around him like a black cocoon, and threw him into the orchestra pit. The xylophone shattered under him. *Plink! Thunk! Crash!*

Dobro turned to say something chivalrous to the ferry keeper's daughter and was surprised to find her staring daggers at him. "How could you!" she snarled through her teeth. "You ruined my show."

Dobro was even more surprised to see a dozen stagehands closing in from all sides. A cabbage, thrown from the audience, whizzed over his head, and an overripe tomato splatted against his shoulder blade.

Soon it was raining rotten vegetables. Dobro was dodging black squash and green sweet potatoes and trying to decide which of the stagehands to whip first when Aidan and Sadie flew into the circle of the stage lights on a second curtain rope and sent two of Dobro's attackers sprawling with two perfectly placed kicks. The three of them shot through the gap before the remaining stagehands closed it, and Sadie led them through the maze of old scenery and props until they found an exit. The theater manager had already sent for the castle guards, who were still in the neighborhood searching for Aidan and Dobro.

Sadie pointed to the low roof of a cottage behind the theater. "That way," she directed. Dobro scrambled up onto the thatch. Aidan climbed up behind him. They had crested the roof and were running down the slope of the other side before they realized Sadie hadn't climbed up with them. Peeking over the ridge of the roof, they saw that she had run in the opposite direction. She was creating a diversion to aid their escape, bouncing paving stones off the helmets of King Darrow's guards.

"Reckon we ought to help her?" Dobro gasped.

"I have a feeling Sadie can take care of herself," Aidan said.

"That gal's got gumption, don't she?" Dobro marveled. "That gal's got what it takes."

The houses in that quarter of Tambluff were close together, and Aidan and Dobro had no trouble running rooftop to rooftop almost all the way to the south gate. The uproar in the city grew as word spread of the strangers who set off the ruckus in the Swan Theater. More torches were lit and more voices raised in shouts; more people wandered into the streets to see any excitement that might come their way.

Aidan and Dobro were a hundred strides from the south gate before they were noticed, running across the roof of the tailor's shop. "There they are!" someone shouted, and a dozen voices joined the chorus. With concealment lost, Aidan knew speed was their only remaining hope. He and Dobro dropped to the ground and pelted the remaining distance as hard as they could go. "The gate!" someone bellowed behind them. "Southporter! Close the gate!"

Through the window of the gatehouse, they could see the short, round silhouette of Southporter heaving away at the wheel that lowered the portcullis. But the portcullis didn't drop. Aidan smiled as he ran. He realized that Southporter was only going through the motions, only pretending to turn the wheel. The instant they were through the gate, it thundered down behind them.

"To the left!" Aidan could hear Southporter shouting to the guards patrolling outside the wall. "They've run into the thicket on the left!" Aidan knew what that meant. He and Dobro lurched to the right. And there, in a copse of low-limbed oak trees, they found their horses—fed, watered, rested, and ready to gallop down the Western Road and toward the safety of Sinking Canyons.

Chapter Twenty

Gully

he Western Road cut through a series of gentle hills just east of the Bonifay Plain. There Aidan and Dobro met a farmer working in a great, deep, red-banked gully that opened onto the road. His son stood in the bed of a wagon drawn by a heavy farm horse. The son heaved sandbags down into the gully where his father stacked them into a knee-high wall that cut across the floor of the gully from one bank to the other.

"Hello," Aidan called. He and Dobro dismounted from their horses. The sweat-slick farmer stopped, wiped his brow with the back of his wrist, and waved. He was glad for the break.

"What you doing?" Dobro asked the farmer.

"Trying to slow down this gully, hopefully save the road from washing out," the farmer answered.

Dobro sighted up the gully. It was a hundred strides long and arrow straight, ten feet deep or more in most places, ten long strides across. Its red-clay banks dropped vertically down to a rocky floor.

"Friend, I believe you got the master gully I ever seen," Dobro announced.

"Why, thank you," the man said with mock modesty. "I dug it myself."

Dobro raised his eyebrow. "Must have takened you a long time."

"Not really," the old farmer said. "I finished in a day."

Dobro whistled. "Mister, I'd surely love to watch you work a shovel."

The man laughed. "I didn't use a shovel. I used a plow."

Dobro gave Aidan a significant look. "See," he said, "I told you working a plow was a dangerous way to pass the time." He looked at the looming walls of the gully. "Veezo hisself couldn't have done this much damage with a plow in a single day."

Aidan laughed and cut a look at the farmer. "He's teasing you, Dobro. He didn't dig this gully, certainly not in a single day."

"I reckon I did too," the farmer shot back. "That ain't the sort of thing I'd lie about. And it sure ain't the sort of thing I'd brag about."

"He's telling true," said the boy before lying back in the bed of the wagon and covering his eyes with a floppy hat. He knew the story his father was about to tell and figured the old boy could tell it fine without his help.

The farmer pointed up the gully. "This is the property line between my farm and my neighbor's—from here up this slope to where those two hills divide. About four years ago, I decided to plow a furrow right down this line to show where my farm ended and his farm began." He made a slicing gesture with his hand, following the line of the gully.

"I knowed to plow a field across the slope, to keep the dirt from washing away. But I didn't figure it would hurt anything to plow two or three furrows straight up this slope."

He shook his head, as if to indicate how wrong he had been. "This here's a natural drain anyway," he said. He swept his hands down to a point to indicate the flow of water off the hills on either side of the gully. "First rainstorm to come through, half the topsoil in my furrow ended up in the road down there. Wasn't many more rains before this gully was cut all the way down to the bedrock. Started widening from there."

They had walked halfway up the gully by now, stepping over little sandbag walls every twenty strides or so. The ground level was a good four feet above their heads. Dobro was looking a little nervous about being "in a gully, down a hole," as the old rhyme put it.

"How long ago did you say you plowed this spot?" Aidan asked.

"Four years ago."

Aidan shook his head slowly. He was amazed so much had happened so quickly.

"But it only took a year or so for it to get this deep," the farmer clarified. "It don't take but a few freshet rains to cut all the way down to bedrock." He stomped his boot on the flat chunk of rock where he stood.

The farmer looked up at the sun. "It's getting late," he said, then he gave a loud whistle for his horse. "If I aim to lay more sandbags today, I better hurry back to the barn for another wagonload." The horse and wagon jangled up to the gully rim, and the farmer climbed up to ground level and into the driver's seat. His son was still asleep in the bed of the wagon.

"Good-bye and good travels," the farmer called as the wagon started moving. "And don't plow down the slope!"

Aidan and Dobro took their time making their way back to the road. There were few really good flinging rocks to be had in Sinking Canyons, and Dobro was filling his pouch with rocks scattered on the gully floor. Aidan enjoyed a few minutes of shade beneath the western bank before they had to get back on their horses. He was crumbling a handful of red clay when he heard a most unexpected sound: *Maaa-aaa-aaah!*

Aidan looked up into the yellow-green eyes of a nanny goat peering over the edge of the gully. The head of a billy goat appeared beside her with its curving horns, and then a spray of white hair and the brown, wrinkled face of Bayard the Truthspeaker.

"Bayard!" Aidan and Dobro shouted in joyful unison. They clambered out of the gully to embrace the old man. He still seemed strong and hearty. *How old must he be now?* thought Aidan.

"What a pleasant surprise!" said Bayard. Aidan wondered, however, if anything ever really surprised the old prophet. "Aidan Errolson and"—he looked over Dobro and pretended to have trouble recognizing him—"Dobro Turtlebane? But you're so pink! Dobro, you haven't gone civilized, have you?"

"Well, I . . ." Dobro began modestly.

"Not nearly as civilized as he thinks," Aidan offered, "though he has become something of a theatergoer."

"If you don't mind my asking," said Bayard, "what are you doing in a gully?"

Dobro said, "Me and Aidan just run up with a sure-enough modern day Veezo, Bayard. Feller says he dug this whole gully with a plow."

Bayard nodded. "I have seen such things before. But what are you doing in this part of the island? I knew the two of you had come out of the Feechiefen. But I thought you were in Sinking Canyons."

"Don't that beat all you ever heard?" asked Dobro. "A feechie living in a big hole in the ground!"

"'Fallen are the Vezeyfolks,'" Bayard quoted. "'In a gully, down a hole. No more fistfights, no more jokes.'" Dobro joined in on the chorus: "'In a gully, down a hole.'"

"Every night I go to sleep with my mama's voice in my head," said Dobro. "'Fallen are the feechiefolks, in a gully, down a hole.' I wake up in the morning, and there I am, down a hole. Ain't no place for feechiefolks, I can tell you."

"But, Bayard," Aidan said, "you said Vezeyfolks. 'Fallen are the Vezeyfolks.'"

"Did I?" Bayard shrugged. "Dobro was talking about Veezo a minute ago. I must have confused 'Veezo' and 'feechiefolks' into 'Vezeyfolks.'"

Aidan eyed Bayard. It wasn't like him to mix up the old lore, whether it was feechie lore or civilizer lore. Was the old prophet starting to lose his wits in his old age?

"I understand you have an army now," Bayard said.

"Yes," Aidan answered.

"You're going to need it. The Pyrthens are coming, you know."

"Is that a prophecy?" Aidan asked. "Or just an observation?"

Bayard smiled. "You don't have to be a prophet to predict that the Pyrthens are coming when a kingdom grows weak. Are you ready to fight?"

"We'll have to be ready, won't we? You make do with what you have." Aidan began to think of everything he and his officers needed to do before the militiamen could really be called a serious fighting force.

"Old Errol's been working them villagers pretty good," Dobro offered. "Marchin', shootin' arrows at just-pretend soldiers, diggin' tunnels. And when they ain't doin' that, Jasper's got them diggin' up timbers and cold-shiny pots and rubbish like that."

Bayard laughed, though he had no idea what Dobro was talking about. "Aidan," he asked, "what's Dobro saying about digging up timbers and pots?"

Aidan was deep in thought about the inevitable battles against the Pyrthens. "Timbers and pots?" he repeated absently. "Oh, that. A flood in the canyons uncovered a piece of a shingled roof. We got to digging around, and we found what appears to be part of two or three cabins, an old plow, some pots and pans."

"Cabins?" Bayard asked. "Why would there be cabins in the Clay Wastes?"

"We was hoping you might be able to tell us, Bayard," Dobro said. "Arliss found a coin the other day had a picture of Harvo Hornhead on it."

"Dobro says it looks like Harvo Hornhead," Aidan said. "I think it looks like Halverd the Antlered, first king of Halverdy. It wasn't a Corenwalder coin, though, or Halverden either. Had the word *Veziland* engraved on it."

Aidan noticed that Bayard was gazing into the gully. He had a faraway look in his eyes. Aidan had seen that look before—on that day, six years earlier, when Bayard came to Longleaf, searching for the Wilderking. The day he foretold that Aidan would be the Wilderking. The old prophet seemed to be in another world. Aidan couldn't tell whether Bayard could even hear what he was saying.

"'Fallen are the Vezeyfolk,'" Bayard muttered, still staring at the opposite bank of the gully. He turned on his heel and strode along the edge of the gully toward the Western Road. His goats trotted to keep up.

"Bayard!" Aidan cried, a little alarmed at the sudden change in the man. "Where are you going?"

"To the library!" Bayard shouted without looking back.

"Wait, Bayard! Come to Sinking Canyons with us!" Aidan called after him. "We need you!"

Bayard didn't answer, but kept walking with the long, fast strides of a man with a purpose.

"Bayard, I need your help!" Aidan was almost begging now, trying to push past the goats to catch up with the Truthspeaker. "I need advice, Bayard."

Bayard kept walking but turned his head to speak. "Live the life that unfolds before you."

"Not that kind of advice, Bayard!"

"Love goodness more than you fear evil."

"No, Bayard! That's what you always tell me. I need some new advice!"

Bayard stopped dead at the edge of the road and turned to face Aidan. "No, Aidan," he said firmly, "you don't need any new advice. You need to heed the old advice."

"But, Bayard, everything has gotten so complicated. I try to lead, but people don't always follow. I try to follow, and nobody seems to be leading. I just don't understand what I'm supposed to—"

Bayard quieted Aidan with a raised hand. "Well then, Aidan, here's my advice: Do what you were doing already. Hurry to Sinking Canyons. Be ready to fight. The Pyrthens are coming."

Aidan nodded.

"Did you need a prophet to tell you that?"

Aidan shook his head no.

"The future is a dark path, Aidan. It's even dark for me most of the time, and I'm a prophet. But the living God always gives you light to get to the next turning. Stay in the path, Aidan. There's light enough. When you get to the second turning, the third, the twentieth, they'll be lit too."

Bayard put a hand on Aidan's shoulder. "You don't need a prophet as much as you think you do, Aidan. You need to live the life the living God is unfolding before you."

Bayard turned to go east, the direction from which Aidan and Dobro had come. Then he turned back for one last word. "This was no chance meeting." He pointed up the gully. "Remember this place. Here is written the history of Corenwald."

Chapter Twenty-One

Gate Stone

Aidan just wanted to rest when he got back to Sinking Canyons. It had been a long trip from Tambluff. But Jasper wouldn't wait. He grabbed Aidan by the arm and began leading him down-canyon. "Aidan!" he said. "You're not going to believe this!"

"Can it wait?" Aidan asked. "I really need to see Father."

"See Father later," Jasper insisted. "You've got to see this."

"Are you taking me to the diggings?" Aidan asked.

Jasper nodded eagerly.

"Jasper, we've got a lot of things to do that are a lot more important than digging up old timbers and broken pottery. You're supposed to be helping train an army."

"I have been helping train an army, Aidan," Jasper retorted, a touch of indignation in his voice. "You're the one who's been gallivanting all over the place."

They soon arrived at the diggings, which were significantly bigger than they had been when Aidan left for Tambluff. "Looks like you've put the new recruits to work," Aidan observed.

"Every good soldier needs to have some practice digging fortifications," Jasper said. "They might as well practice here."

"But this is what I wanted to show you," Jasper continued. He pointed at a blue-gray granite block, about two feet in height, depth, and width.

"You dug this up?" Aidan asked.

"Yes. It took eight men to drag it out of the hole."

Aidan marveled at the great block of granite. What kind of flood brought it into the canyon? "It looks almost like a gate stone," he said.

"It is a gate stone," said Jasper. "Look at this." He tapped the far side of the stone.

Aidan walked around to that side of the stone, where he saw an inscription: "New Vezey."

"Didn't I say you wouldn't believe it?" Jasper whooped.

"New Vezey," Aidan read again. "What is New Vezey?"

"It's carved on a village gate stone, so we figure

it's the name of a village," Jasper answered. "But nobody's heard of a village called New Vezey. We've got men from all over Corenwald here, and I think I've asked every one of them. But nobody knows of a place called New Vezey."

"And nothing from the old lore?"

"There was a village registry among the manuscripts I brought from the library at Longleaf, but it makes no mention of New Vezey."

Aidan concentrated on those words, *New Vezey*. Something was on the tip of his tongue, but it just wouldn't come.

"So what do you think?" Jasper asked.

Aidan raised his hand for silence. "New Vezey," he mumbled, his eyes closed, "New Vezey . . . Vezey . . . Vezey . . . Vezey . . ."

Suddenly, Aidan's eyes popped open, and he raised an index finger. He recited:

Oh, Veezo, you is ruint,
Covered up in clay.
With choppin' and plowin'
You tore up the ground
And now it's washed away.

"What are you talking about?" Jasper asked. His expression showed genuine alarm, as if he thought his brother had gone crazy.

"Dobro's sadballad," Aidan answered. "About Veezo and the magical plow." He repeated the stanza again:

Oh, Veezo, you is ruint,
Covered up in clay.
With choppin' and plowin'
You tore up the ground
And now it's washed away.

"I think that legend might tell what happened here."

Jasper stared at his brother. *Yes*, he thought, *he's finally lost his wits.*

Aidan looked up at the band of red clay just below the canyon rim. He rested his fingers horizontally across the bridge of his nose to shield the rest of the canyon wall from his vision. "Pretend there's no canyon here," he told Jasper. "Pretend there's just a clay bank cut into the ground."

Jasper shielded his own vision the way Aidan had and gazed up at the bank.

"Have you ever seen anything that looked like that?" Aidan asked.

"Just looks like a plain old gully when you look at it that way," said Jasper.

"Dobro and I saw one yesterday. A man had plowed a furrow straight down a slope instead of terracing across it."

"Not very smart," Jasper observed.

"That was only four years ago. Four years of rains washing down that slope, and that furrow has become a gully you can't jump across. Every bit of topsoil has washed away, off down the hill somewhere. Topsoil ten feet deep, all the way down to the bedrock, just gone."

"I still don't see what you're getting at," Jasper said.

"Let's say you put a farm—no, not a farm, a whole village—on a spot where that nice red topsoil isn't sitting on bedrock or hardpacked clay but on a layer of sand and loose clay a hundred feet thick." Aidan pointed straight up in the air, where he imagined this village might have once stood. "And let's say there's a farmer whose fields border the village, and he plows his furrows the wrong way—down the slope, not across it.

"When the topsoil is gone from that farmer's field, can you imagine how quickly the sand below it would wash out? You saw how much sand and clay moved through here in a single rainstorm."

Jasper looked as if he was starting to get the picture. "So you're saying this farmer is the Veezo from Dobro's story?"

"No, I'm saying the song isn't about a man named Veezo. It's about a village called New Vezey. It must have gotten garbled through the years. It wasn't a farmer who got swallowed up by the clay. It was a whole village. This gate stone, these timbers, the plow blade didn't wash up. They fell down, just like that pine tree did."

Jasper wasn't yet ready to accept all of Aidan's theory. "It just doesn't make sense, Aidan."

"It makes more sense than any other explanation we've come up with," Aidan insisted. "It explains a lot of the feechies' peculiar ways. Think about how many superstitions Dobro has about this place."

"Time to leave these neighborhoods," Jasper mimicked in his best Dobro voice.

"Exactly," said Aidan. "Probably the worst disaster in the history of feechiedom. A whole village abandoned, then swallowed up by the earth. Even if they don't exactly remember what happened here, you can imagine the superstitions that would grow up around this place."

"Dobro did say the feechies started out as farmers and villagers," Jasper remembered.

Aidan raised both hands to gesture at his surroundings. "And then *this* happens. No wonder they gave up farming and took to the forest. This is what made them feechiefolk."

"I've just got one more question," said Jasper. "Why would farmers—even bad farmers—try to farm the Clay Wastes?"

Aidan shrugged. "Maybe they weren't Clay Wastes three hundred years ago. Maybe they only became Clay Wastes after the topsoil washed away."

Jasper smiled. "Perhaps it was for the best that the feechies gave up farming. There may not have been any topsoil left on this island by the time the civilizers got here."

Chapter Twenty-Two

A Skirmish

Three weeks after Aidan and Dobro returned from Tambluff, a convoy of Pyrthen ships landed at Middenmarsh and disgorged four legions—twenty-four thousand fighting men. They took the port city without any real resistance and, after leaving a small occupying force behind, began raking eastward toward Tambluff. As they marched, they burned the farms and villages along the Western Road.

It was not a complete surprise, therefore, when Ottis ran up to the washing pool from his guard post at the mouth of the canyon. "Pyrthens!" he called. "Pyrthens! A troop of Pyrthens is headed this way!"

"Are you sure they're Pyrthens?" Errol asked.

"Yes, sir," Ottis answered. "I've seen enough Pyrthens to know them when I see them. Black-and-red battle standards. Black armor."

"I suppose you do know a Pyrthen when you see one," said Errol. "How many men?"

"A hundred or so, on horseback."

"A hundred," Errol repeated. "A small cavalry unit."

"Why would they be coming this way?" Brennus asked. "We're twenty leagues off the Western Road."

"They must have heard about rebels holed up in the canyons," Aidan surmised. "They've sent a party to find out whether we're friend or foe."

"I can answer that easily enough," said Errol, instinctively feeling for the sword at his left hip. "How long before they get here, Ottis?"

"A quarter hour at the most," he answered.

Errol began giving orders. "Percy," he said, "you go up the canyon and alert the main camp. We'd rather hide than fight if we can help it, at least until we know what we're up against." He gave Percy a little push in the direction of the camp. "Brennus," he continued, "I want archers on the canyon rim. Fifty here"—he pointed to a stand of trees above them—"and fifty on the north rim. And stay hidden." Brennus sprinted off to do his duty.

Errol pointed to the brushy pine boughs stacked nearby. "Start covering our tracks," he said. "Even if we can't hide the fact that we've been here, we can at least keep the Pyrthens from knowing how many of us there are."

Down the canyon he could see a cloud of dust rising. The Pyrthens would be coming around the bend any minute. "To the caves and crevices," Errol ordered, not quite so loudly. "I don't want to fight unless we have to, not this time. I don't yet want the Pyrthens to know the full extent of our presence here.

But if we have to fight—well, I won't make a speech. You know what we're fighting for."

The men looked at Errol. The light of battle shone in his eyes, and he was beautiful. They all knew what Errol meant. If they had to fight, they would fight for Corenwald, even if it didn't feel like Corenwald anymore. The old man loved Corenwald; that was reason enough to love it, even if they had somehow forgotten how to love Corenwald for its own sake.

Silently, dragging pine boughs behind to cover their tracks, the men disappeared into the folds of the canyon walls behind them. Aidan and Dobro hid behind a dirt chimney that stood nearby. Errol and Jasper tucked themselves behind a clay wall that spurred out from the canyon wall.

They could hear the Pyrthens picking their way through the canyon's maze well before they could see them. The Pyrthens were less than fifty strides away when they emerged from behind the nearest turning of the canyon wall. They were all on horseback, except for the man who led them. He was dressed in the rags of a slave. His bushy beard and wild, matted hair created a sharp contrast to the clean-shaven, close-cropped men who trailed behind him in tight formation. He kept his eyes on the ground; any tracker-guide would keep his eyes on the ground, and that was obviously what this man was. But Aidan could tell from the man's shambling, defeated gait that he always looked at the ground. Still-oozing lash marks were visible through the holes in his tattered garment. His frame was broad; he should have been a big man. But hunger had gotten the better of him. He was mostly bone and skin.

Aidan somehow knew that the slave was a Corenwalder, perhaps a sailor captured by Pyrthen pirates or a mercenary captured in one of Pyrth's unending wars. His heart went out to this country-man, forced to betray his own people by leading the enemy to their doorstep.

The shaggy, stooping slave stopped near the washing pool. "I have led you to Sinking Canyons," he said. His voice was husky with thirst, but there was no mistaking his Corenwalder accent. "Now, by the general's orders, you're supposed to set me free."

The Pyrthen commander looked over the scene. "You were to lead me to the rebel camp. I don't see any rebels."

"These canyons are vast and complex." The slave spoke with some heat, though he never looked into the face of the commander. "I have no more idea than you do where the rebels are. My orders were to lead you to Sinking Canyons. That is what I have done."

The commander's mailed fist sent the Corenwalder slave sprawling to the ground. He snarled, "I'll say what your orders are, you dog."

The slave stood to his feet. Aidan noticed with great admiration that he didn't even rub the cheek the Pyrthen had struck. "The general," the slave began. "The general's orders—you were to set me free when

I had led you to Sinking Canyons. I have served him these three years."

The commander laughed a cruel, mocking laugh. "Did you really think the general would set you free? You? A traitor to your own people?"

"My treachery served the general well enough," said the slave.

The commander shrugged. "That may be. But the general thinks no more highly of you than your people, the ones you betrayed, must think of you. Neither do I, when it comes to it."

"But the general's orders . . ." the slave began, a little more hoarsely.

"The general's orders were to kill you once we got to Sinking Canyons." From the pleased look on the commander's face, it was obvious he was telling the truth. "One never knows when a traitor will turn again."

Despairing, the Corenwalder fell to his knees as the Pyrthen slid from his horse and unsheathed his sword. "I am betrayed," he moaned.

The Pyrthen raised his sword and spoke. "It is no treachery to betray a traitor."

Before the Pyrthen's sword fell on the slave's wretched neck, the canyon walls echoed with the voice of Errol, bellowing the name of his long-lost son like a war cry: "Ma-a-ay-n-a-a-a-ard!"

The old man appeared from his hiding place and closed on the Pyrthen with his broadsword raised above his head. He brought his weapon down on the seam of the Pyrthen's black armor, where the shoulder plate met the breastplate. Ten Pyrthens were off their horses before Errol freed his blade for a second stroke. A quick, vicious thrust from an officer's sword sent Errol to the ground. Arrows whistling down from the canyon rim felled a dozen horsemen. A second volley of arrows dropped a dozen more Pyrthens before the first wave of Corenwalder swordsmen fell on the enemy, making it impossible for the archers to go on shooting.

The Battle of Sinking Canyons was terrible. The Pyrthens were ruthless and efficient fighters. They hurt and killed their share of Corenwalders. But they were hugely outnumbered by the militiamen who appeared from the canyon's every crack and crevice, like ants boiling out of the hidden holes of an anthill. Corenwalders circling around from the canyon mouth sealed off the invaders' only escape route, but still the Pyrthens wouldn't surrender. Three or four Pyrthens burst through the lines, dodged the archers' arrows, and galloped to safety. The rest spilled their lifeblood on the sands of Sinking Canyons.

Soon after the fighting broke out, Maynard dragged his father to the safety of a small cave. For the slave who had led the Pyrthens to Sinking Canyons was, of course, Maynard, the second of Errol's sons, who had once tried to pass himself off as the Wilderking in the Feechiefen Swamp. As the battle raged outside, Maynard held his dying father in the cool darkness and wept for the years he had wasted, for the sins he had committed against the father who had traded his own life for the life of a son who betrayed him.

While his life was ebbing away, Errol opened his eyes. When he saw his son, a faint smile flickered across his face. "Maynard," he said. In spite of his weakness, the voice that spoke the name of his son was so strong with love and tenderness it seemed to bear away all the hurt that had passed between the two of them. "Maynard, you were never meant to be a slave."

Chapter Twenty-Three

An End
and a Beginning

The Pyrthens were coming. Surely they would be coming after those few escaped horsemen returned to the main body of the army. The Pyrthens knew where the rebels were, knew how many they were, and knew that they were enemies.

There was no time to bury the dead with the honors the fighting men would have liked to accord to their fallen brothers. They placed the dead in tunnels—the Corenwalders in one chamber, the Pyrthens in another—and sealed them in.

The Errolsons buried their father in his own grave, out of the canyon in the plain above; they felt sure he would prefer to be buried in more solid ground than that of the canyons. Aidan, Percy, Jasper, and Brennus stood around their father's grave while Aidan offered up a prayer of thanks for their father's life. Maynard hung back a few steps, wanting to honor his father but not sure how welcome he would be among his brothers.

By the time Aidan had finished his prayer, Maynard was crying violent tears. He squatted on the ground, his bony arms folded around his knees, and rocked back and forth on his heels. His hoarse wailing echoed across the plain and off the canyon walls a hundred strides away.

Brennus opened his eyes and glared at his brother. "A little late for that, isn't it, Maynard?"

"Brennus . . ." Aidan began, reproach in his voice.

"Don't 'Brennus' me, Aidan. Does that howling do any honor to Father? It's no more than the self-pity of a son who broke Father's heart a thousand times over. A son who brought the enemy to our front porch, who betrayed thirty-six hundred men, the least of whom is more worthy than he. The son who was the direct cause of Father's death. No, I don't see how those tears honor Father at all."

Maynard's tears of shame and sorrow flowed all the more. His wailing grew louder, shriller.

"Brennus," said Aidan quietly, "if you wish to honor Father, then love what Father loved."

Brennus stomped off without another word, waving a hand behind him. Percy and Jasper weren't so violent as Brennus in their reactions. But they weren't yet ready to receive Maynard into the bosom of the family either. They, too, wandered off in the direction of the canyons.

Aidan squatted down beside his older brother and put his arm around him until he stopped his wailing. The two of them walked to the rim of the canyon, still not speaking, and sat with their feet dangling from the edge. They watched the daily activities of thirty-five hundred men, below, getting on with their lives. Men were bathing their wounds in the wash pool, starting fires to cook their evening meals, talking in little groups.

To their left, the sun was going down, the brilliant purples and pinks of its dying light magnifying the colors that swirled in the canyon walls.

They sat that way for five minutes or more before Maynard finally spoke. "His love haunted me, you know. All the way across the ocean it haunted me." He watched a pebble bounce down the side of the cliff.

"False love I could handle. Flattery, using people, even being used—I understood all that. That made sense to me. But unconditional love was the last thing I wanted, from Father or anybody else. Because to receive unconditional love is to know somebody loves you more than you deserve to be loved.

"I don't mean Father ever meant to make me feel unworthy. I don't even think he knew he loved me more than I deserved. I just mean a love that intense can't help but make you see your own selfishness.

"So I spent my life trying to prove I deserved more

than I was getting. That's why I tried to pass myself off as the Wilderking. Who's more deserving than a king?

"When that didn't work, I went to Pyrth. I had something they wanted, and I thought they would honor me for it. I could help give them victory over Corenwald, the one kingdom they had never been able to conquer. I could come home a victor, not groveling for Father's forgiveness but making him grovel for mine.

"But the Pyrthens didn't love me. They broke me. They made me a slave, not a general. Then, when it was too late, I understood I needed unconditional love more than I needed anything in the world."

He began to weep again but softly this time, not violently as before. "I was sure I had finally put myself beyond Father's love. But after all those years, after all that hurt, it finally tracked me down. And it saved me."

"He never slackened in his love for you," Aidan said after a long silence. "I can tell you that." He looked down into the canyon, which was now growing dark. "And now he's gone. I can't get my mind around it. It's as if we woke up one morning back home and found that the River Tam was gone. Some things you just figure will always be there."

He waved his hand out over the canyon. "You know, a village used to stand there."

Maynard pointed down at the canyon floor. "Down there?" he asked, surprised to hear that anyone would put a village in the bottom of Sinking Canyons.

"No," said Aidan, pointing again. "Out there. It stood right out there, in a spot that's now a hundred feet in the air. It was solid ground then, and the villagers built solid little cabins on it. They cooked their suppers, raised their children, visited with their neighbors. On nights like this, they stepped out their doors and watched the sun go down.

"And then the earth opened up and swallowed their little village. Which goes to show, you'd better be careful what you put your faith in. The things of earth look mighty solid, mighty permanent. But then they go away."

The diggings were just visible in the failing light. "We found part of that village, by the way," Aidan said, lest Maynard think he was making it up, or maybe speaking figuratively. "Dug it up with shovels. The name of that solid little village was right there on the gate stone: New Vezey."

Maynard got a strange look on his face. "Did you say New Vezey?"

"That's right," said Aidan. "We think it was an old feechie settlement."

Maynard paused, deep in thought. When he finally spoke, he spoke slowly, carefully. "The Pyrthens have a saying: *Until New Vezey rises, the Empire will stand.*"

Aidan looked perplexed at the odd saying.

"It's like saying the Pyrthen Empire will stand until pigs fly or until the stars fall from the sky," Maynard explained. "It means the empire will stand forever."

Aidan shook his head. "I still don't understand."

"There's a legend people tell on the continent about the Vezians, or Vezeyfolk. They were a warrior tribe that lived in a broad river valley they called Vezey Land."

"Veziland," Aidan muttered, remembering the inscription on the coin that Arliss found.

"When the Pyrthen empire first rose to power," Maynard said, "the Vezeyfolk were one of the tribes they conquered. Vezeyfolk were driven out of Vezey Land, and their king, Halverd the Antlered, led them into the country that came to be called Halverdy. Which is where our people came from."

"The Halverdens started out as Vezeyfolk?" Aidan asked. "I never knew this." Indeed, even the most learned of Corenwald's lore masters were a little hazy on the history of the Halverdens before they came to Corenwald.

"All that part is historical fact," Maynard continued. "But then there's the legend of New Vezey. According to the legend, King Halverd sent a select group of Vezeyfolk over the ocean to establish a colony called New Vezey, just in case they put them on ships and waved good-bye, and that was the last anybody ever saw of the New Vezians. They were shipwrecked on an island somewhere. Then, according to the legend, the earth just opened up and swallowed them.

"Just fairy-tale talk, of course. Just a legend. That's why the Pyrthens say their empire will stand until

New Vezey rises again, because there never was any New Vezey."

"But there was," Aidan said, his voice rising with excitement. "There was a New Vezey, and we found it. Vezeyfolk . . ." Aidan muttered. "Feechiefolk . . . Vezey . . . feechie . . ." He remembered Bayard's misquoted rhyme: "'Fallen are the Vezeyfolk . . .'" He remembered Bayard's sudden realization that sent him running for the library.

"The feechiefolk are Vezeyfolk," Maynard said, the realization slowly dawning on him. "They're descended from the lost colony."

"Yes!" said Aidan, nearly shouting. "Descended from the same people we're descended from. That explains why we found a Vezilander coin in the diggings. Their Harvo Hornhead is our Halverd the Antlered. That explains why they speak our language."

The realization made him almost giddy. "The feechies are our people, Maynard! We're one tribe!"

"*The empire stands until New Vezey rises again,*" Maynard quoted. "So the Pyrthens have better reason to hate us than they know: We are New Vezians, together with the feechiefolk. If only we can rise again."

Aidan understood a new truth about the Wilderking prophecy: The Wilderking wouldn't merely unite the feechies and the civilizers into a single kingdom. He would *reunite* them, two parts of a single tribe that had been separated for three centuries.

Chapter Twenty-Four

Preparations

Days passed, and the expected attack by the Pyrthens didn't come. News of the invasion soon came, however, and it wasn't good. Tambluff had fallen. Much of the city had burned, and Tambluff Castle was now inhabited by Pyrthen officers.

Rather than allow the Pyrthens to besiege Tambluff and subject its inhabitants to starvation and disease, the Corenwalder army had given the Pyrthens battle outside the city walls, led by King Darrow and Prince Steren. The Corenwalder army was scattered to the four winds. King Darrow was killed in the battle. It was believed Prince Steren survived—or King Steren now, if indeed he did survive.

"They will surely be coming now," said Aidan to his brothers. "And they will bring the main body of their force. This is the only army they have left to fight against."

To Aidan's surprise, however, the Pyrthen army wasn't the first army to arrive at Sinking Canyons. Word had gone out among Corenwald's scattered warriors that resistance to the Pyrthen occupation would center on Sinking Canyons and Aidan Errolson's army. They streamed in for a day and a half, in groups of ten, fifteen, fifty. Sometimes whole units came. Civilians came, men who had no part in the battle at Tambluff but had heard about Sinking Canyons and wanted to play a role. Some came believing Steren was king. Others came believing Aidan would be king, believing they were among the first recruits of the Wilderking's army. Indeed, many of these stragglers suspected the Sinking Canyons army would be mostly feechies.

With every new group that came, Aidan studied the faces, hoping Steren was among them. And at last, the fourth morning after the Tambluff battle, Steren rode up at the head of a cavalry unit, a dashing figure on a black horse.

Aidan bowed before his old friend. "King Steren! You are welcome to Sinking Canyons. We are yours to command."

Steren leaped from his horse and, pulling Aidan to his feet, embraced him as a brother.

"I am sorry to hear about your father," said Aidan. "We are all sorry."

"Thank you," Steren said. "He was beautiful, Aidan. I wish you could have seen him on that last day. He was first in the attack and last in the retreat. He was worthy of Corenwald that day, Aidan, and I shall always remember him that way, astride his black horse, tilting toward the enemy."

"Then I will remember him that way too," said Aidan.

"The Pyrthens aren't far behind me," said Steren. "They'll start arriving later today. They may attack as early as tomorrow. I need to review the troops immediately so we can prepare for battle. How many men do we have?"

"Seven or eight thousand foot soldiers," Aidan answered. "Then there's your cavalry unit and a second cavalry unit we've cobbled together from individual horsemen who have arrived in the last two days and men riding horses captured from the Pyrthens."

"Seven or eight thousand," Steren mused. "The enemy is probably twice that at least. Well then, we shall make do with what we have."

The rest of the day was spent in preparation for the coming battle. Scouts gave the officers a tour of the canyons' terrain. King Steren organized the new recruits into makeshift units and assigned them to officers. Late in the afternoon, the scouts at the canyon rim reported the arrival of the first Pyrthen units on the north side of the canyon. The Pyrthens kept coming well into the night.

Outside the tunnel complex, the five Errolsons and Dobro sat in a circle with King Steren. There were no fires on the canyon floor that night. Men circled around fires would have made easy targets for the Pyrthen archers, who were surely in position already at the north rim of the canyon. The Corenwalder scouts on the south rim could see hundreds and hundreds of

Pyrthen campfires flickering across the plain on the other side.

Aidan was explaining his plan to the others. "We could hold these canyons forever if we had to," he said. "Archers can't really hurt us. Any archer who was in position to shoot down on us from the rim would be very exposed himself. We could pick them off like flies.

"They'd have to come in after us, down to the canyon floor. And they couldn't roust us out that way even if they had a hundred thousand men. We know every crevice of these canyons and every hidey-hole. They'd be fighting an invisible enemy. We could ambush them from a different spot every day."

"They could starve us out," Brennus observed.

"We could attack their supply trains, carry off their food," Aidan said. "We could eat better than they do."

"Fine," Steren said. "We can hold the canyons. Then what? The Pyrthens have Corenwald's army contained in Sinking Canyons. As long as they get to keep the rest of Corenwald, I think they'll be happy to make that trade."

"But don't you see?" Aidan said. "From here we could wreak havoc on the Pyrthens. Their supply train will have to stretch from Middenmarsh all the way to Tambluff. Our raiding parties could hit them anywhere on the Western Road, then beat it back here to the canyons. We can organize resistance in the villages, create a whole country of insurgents. Eventually we could win Corenwald back."

"Eventually?" Steren said. "Eventually? Aidan, you're still thinking like an outlaw: Hide out, bide your time, wait for something good to happen. Eventually!" He nearly spat the word. "Meanwhile, our people are living under the oppression of the Pyrthens. That's no way for my people to live, Aidan. I am king of Corenwald. I won't lead an insurgency in my own kingdom. We're not a band of outlaws. We're an army. We're the army of Corenwald."

But Aidan had spent a lot of time planning his insurgency. He had also dug a lot of tunnels. He wasn't ready to give up so easily. "We know every nook and cranny of these canyons," he said, his voice rising. "Do you have any idea of the advantage—"

King Steren raised a finger to his lips for quiet. "What's that sound?" he asked. All night they had heard the murmur of Pyrthen voices and the jingle of horse tack, the occasional clank of weapons being moved or stacked. But now there were new noises coming from the northern rim—great metallic groans and iron squeaks, the blowing and stamping of horses under strain, the barks of the horse masters.

Maynard had heard these sounds many times before in his travels with the Pyrthen army. "Gun carriages," he said. "They're putting gun carriages in place."

The term was unfamiliar to the Corenwalders. "Remember the thunder-tubes the Pyrthens used at Bonifay?" he said. "The Pyrthens call them cannons. They're lining them up on the other rim." The moon hadn't risen yet, but by starlight the Corenwalders could just make out the silhouettes of men, horses, and thunder-tubes on the canyon rim directly across from them. A peninsula of land jutted out into the canyon, a huge semicircular stage with the canyon for an orchestra pit. Teams of draft horses pulled a dozen guns close to the edge, where the foot lanterns would be if it really were a stage.

"They've done a good scouting job," Percy remarked. "They seem to know our position exactly."

"We can't hold this position," said Maynard.

"We can go deep in the tunnels . . ." Aidan began, but Maynard just shook his head.

"We could hold these canyons forever against archers, infantry, cavalry—against any fighting force we Corenwalders are used to fighting against. But you haven't considered what cannons can do to a place like this. Those iron balls will pulverize this canyon wall. These tunnels will collapse at the first impact. Anybody inside will be buried alive. Those who are outside will have one less place to hide. I saw those cannoneers blow a rocky cliff to bits on one of the eastern isles, where pirates were hiding. That was solid granite. You don't want to see what they could do to this sand and clay."

Aidan envisioned his own hopes and plans blown away by the Pyrthen guns like the pirates' granite hideout.

"We'll split the army," Steren announced without any preamble.

"We'll what?" asked Aidan.

"We'll split the army for a night march. Aidan, you'll lead half the men and one cavalry unit up the canyon. I'll lead the rest of the men and the other cavalry unit down the canyon. What is it, a league upstream to the end of the canyon?"

"A league and a half," said Jasper.

"And a little less than that to the downstream end, if I remember correctly," said Steren. "Aidan, when you get out of the canyon, you'll double back along the canyon rim, or as close as you can get without attracting the sentries' notice. I'll do the same thing from the other end.

"In the morning, when they open up those thunder-tubes on this spot, you boys will hit them on their right flank, and we'll hit them on their left."

"Like a pair of tongs," said Brennus.

"Exactly," Steren answered. "This is no time to be playing defense. If we can engage the enemy, they can't use their thunder-tubes without shooting into their own men. If everything goes well, we can just fold them up, back their right flank into their left flank. Then they'll have to fight us in front and behind at the same time."

Aidan shook his head. "You're talking about some sort of last stand?"

Steren shrugged. "I hope not. No, I'm talking about winning this battle."

"But, Steren, we're such a small force already. I just don't think splitting up is a good idea."

"Aidan, I have already had your advice, and I thank you for it. Now I need your obedience." He was every bit a king.

"Yes," said Aidan. "Yes, Your Majesty."

Chapter Twenty-Five

A Battle

The moon rose after midnight to light the way for the Corenwalders as they made their way to either end of the canyon. It was only a quarter moon, but the white walls of the canyon reflected every bit of its light; for the men who knew the canyon, it was more than enough light. The newcomers who didn't know the canyon followed the men who did.

The Corenwalders were in their positions well before daylight. A little wet-weather creek paralleled the right flank of the sleeping Pyrthens, about fifty strides away. It was lined by scraggly bushes that stood about as high as a man's chest. Here, behind the bushes, Aidan and his four thousand men waited for daylight to come.

The sun had barely appeared over the lower canyon horizon when the Pyrthen thunder-tubes opened up on what, just a few hours earlier, had been the Corenwalder position. The earth shuddered with the explosions in the cannons' mouths, and the smoke from the burning powder hung over the canyon. Great chunks of earth fell from the canyon wall to the floor after the first volley. By the second or third volley, the dust thrown up by the cave-ins made it impossible to see the other side of the canyon. Had the Corenwalders stayed in the canyons, any of those who survived the cave-ins would surely have suffocated in the dust.

The Pyrthen soldiers crowded near the canyon's edge to watch the catastrophe, cheering raucously at what they believed to be the destruction of the last remaining enemy. The sight convinced them they would not be fighting that day.

A few of the Pyrthens saw the Corenwalders coming. A few on the right who had lost interest in the pounding of Sinking Canyons saw Aidan running toward them, his mouth stretched in a primal shout, with four thousand men behind him. A few on the left saw King Steren leading his men across the last few strides before they collided with the outer ring of Pyrthen soldiers. The sentries on both sides called warnings, but nobody heard them over the booming of the cannons. Hundreds of Pyrthens were struck down or hurled from the canyon rim before they had even drawn their swords.

The Corenwalders made remarkable progress in the initial surprise of their attack. For a minute it appeared as if the two halves of the Corenwalder army would snap shut on the two Pyrthen flanks like the jaws of an alligator.

But the Pyrthens were battle hardened, the veterans of many campaigns in many different settings. They soon regained their composure; though by the time they did, their numerical advantage wasn't quite so overwhelming. The officers finally got the cannoneers to hold their fire, allowing them to better communicate orders to their men.

The Pyrthen cavalry mounted horses and were quite effective at scattering the foot soldiers until the Corenwalder cavalry collided with them. Otherwise, the combat was strictly hand to hand, carried out with sword, ax, and spear. The Corenwalders fought desperately in defense of their homeland; they had more to fight for than the Pyrthens did, and that was an advantage. However, the skill and strength of the Pyrthens soon began to show against the Corenwalders, most of whom were farmers and laborers instead of career soldiers.

Dobro fought in a manner worthy of the feechie-folk. In close combat like this, he was easily worth five civilizer soldiers. Maynard, too, fought like a man possessed, understanding for the first time what it meant to fight for Corenwald.

In the midst of the melee, the cannoneers and their horses turned the great gun carriages around and rolled them to the base of the peninsula, away from the rim. They aimed the guns in the direction of the skirmishers, against the remote possibility they would need to fire them.

The two lines of Pyrthen fighters were soon gaining back the ground they had lost, pushing the Corenwalders backward and opening the jaws of the alligator. More and more Corenwalders fell beneath the skillful swords of the Pyrthens.

The Corenwalders' only real hope of victory lay in meeting each other in the middle, forcing the Pyrthens to defend themselves from Corenwalders in front of them and Corenwalders in back of them at the same time. That would have multiplied the Corenwalders' strength. But the farther apart the two skirmish lines got, the more the Corenwalders' strength was divided. Not having succeeded in the initial attack, the Corenwalder army was in danger of being flanked itself. Should that happen, all would be lost.

That appeared to be exactly what was happening to Aidan and his men when Aidan looked up and saw a horse sweeping down from the north, ridden by Bayard the Truthspeaker. His white hair was blown back against his head, and in his right hand he raised a sword. Behind him charged a whole army of feechie-folk—thousands of them. Gray-skinned, turtle-helmeted, bedecked in their gator-hide breastplates, wolf-paw necklaces, and spoonbill feathers, they looked like the swamp itself, come to life and ready to sweep the invaders into Sinking Canyons. They raised stone-tipped spears and kept coming, yodeling, barking, and screaming like wildcats: "Haaa-www-weeeeee!"

The feechies funneled down between the two skirmish lines. Seeing that help had come, the Corenwalders fought with renewed vigor.

The Pyrthens' hearts melted. Many of these same Pyrthens had been at the Battle of Bonifay Plain, when the feechies had routed them in the Eechihoolee Forest. These feechies inspired the same irrational fear that had overwhelmed the Pyrthens six years earlier.

The feechies destroyed those Pyrthens who did not succeed in running away from them. As Pyrthens fell, feechies picked up their curved, cold-shiny swords to use on the next Pyrthen. Some feechies wielded two Pyrthen swords, one in each hand. They were terrifying, the stuff of Pyrthen nightmares.

All of the vaunted Pyrthen discipline broke down completely in the face of the feechies. A few Pyrthens broke through to the open plain, but the great majority of them were funneled down toward the canyon rim. Corenwalders drove them back, back, back against the mouths of the thunder-tubes.

In their desperate panic, Pyrthen officers ordered their cannoneers to fire into the melee. The first round of cannon fire was devastating. The fleeing Pyrthens absorbed much of the damage, but many Corenwalders—both feechie and civilizer—fell in the blasts. The cannon fire didn't stop the Pyrthens from retreating, as their officers had hoped it would. They were still more terrified of the feechies than the cannons, and they ran straight into the cannons' mouths.

The cannon fire did have the effect of slowing the Corenwalder pursuit. The fleeing Pyrthens didn't even notice, but kept streaming onto that big half-moon of land where the guns were placed. Soon all the Pyrthens who didn't lie dead or wounded in the field were cowering behind the guns on the peninsula. They were packed shoulder to shoulder, thousands of them, and some of the men on the perimeter were jostled off into the canyon, where they fell to their deaths. But behind the guns, they were safe from the feechies.

The earth was shaking with the force of the cannon fire. The feechies had been put to confusion amid the smoke and the noise, and the civilizers were only a little better able to keep their heads. Aidan understood they would have to take the guns if they were to have any hope of winning the battle. But that would come only with great loss of Corenwalder life. He needed to find Steren, but the field was shrouded in smoke. He couldn't hear himself think amid the chaos of the cannonade. He had no idea how many of his men were still alive. At any moment the barrage could stop and the Pyrthens could come pouring back over whatever shell-shocked Corenwalders remained.

The cannon fire didn't stop. The earth continued to shake with the force of it. Aidan blundered through the smoke, trying to gather up men to take those guns.

But then came a cannon blast that set off a thunder and shake such as Aidan had never heard before. When the roar began, the sound of the cannons stopped, as if swallowed up by it. The screams of ten thousand men rose above the roar and then they faded, too, as if carried swiftly away. A great rush of air sucked the cannon smoke into the canyon, then belched it back up into a towering billow of dust and smoke.

The Pyrthens were gone. The cannons were gone. The whole peninsula had shaken loose with the vibrations of the thunder-tubes and fallen into the canyon, carrying the Pyrthen army with it.

A hush fell over the battlefield. The men knew they had witnessed a miracle, and their sense of awe did not allow them to speak. Even Dobro had nothing to say. Many Corenwalders were dead and dying on the field—both civilizer and feechie—but not nearly as many as Aidan had feared from the intensity of the cannon fire. That alone would have been miracle enough to make them all fall silent.

"The living God has delivered us this day," said Aidan. "Praise be to the living God, who has delivered Corenwald."

All across the field, men were looking for comrades and brothers. There were many joyful reunions, many tearful good-byes. Aidan rejoiced to find all his brothers safe and sound. Dobro was also unhurt. Aidan's check on his men was interrupted by the feechies who swarmed around him, eager to greet the civilizer hero and feechiefriend.

A messenger pushed his way through the feechies to tell Aidan that King Steren needed to see him immediately. Aidan followed the boy at a gallop across the area that used to be the Pyrthens' left flank. Aidan could tell at a glance that Steren's half of the army had suffered greater losses than his had.

The messenger stopped at a spot where men were kneeling in a circle. Some were sobbing loudly, others were praying. In the center of the circle, King Steren lay broken and bleeding, the casualty of a Pyrthen cannonball.

Aidan leaned down over the fallen king. With great effort, Steren raised a hand and held it in front of Aidan's face as if giving a benediction. "Aidan, you have fulfilled your duty to the House of Darrow," he rasped. "Now do your duty to Corenwald. They would have you for their king." The light was ebbing from his eyes. "The living God has been good to me. I have lived to see Corenwald's deliverance. Hail." He gave a dying gasp. "Hail to the Wilderking." Steren's hand of blessing dropped to his chest, his eyes closed, and the pain on his face melted into an expression of peaceful rest.

Bayard had come running when he heard of King Steren's injury. He reached through the circle of men and placed two fingers on Steren's neck, feeling for a pulse. "The king is dead," he said. "Long live the Wilderking."

Epilogue

After Bayard the Truthspeaker had left Aidan and Dobro at the gulley on the Western Road, he went straight to the library at Tambluff University. There he consulted some long-forgotten scrolls and pieced together the story of the Vezeyfolk and the first, ill-fated human habitation on the island of Corenwald.

He left immediately for the Feechiefen. There, in the largest swamp counsel ever convened, he told the feechiefolk their story—that they and the civilizers were actually one big tribe, all descended from the Vezeyfolk. They had come to Corenwald in two separate waves of immigration, but they had come for the same reason: to escape the aggression of the Pyrthens, to live in a new land in the way they saw fit to live.

At first, the feechies were troubled by Bayard's story. They were a clannish people, and their fierce loyalty to tribe and family had always made them deeply suspicious of the civilizers. They had to change their whole way of thinking as the meaning of Bayard's story became clear to them. Now, rather than separating them from the civilizers, the feechies' clannishness suddenly bound them to the civilizers as brothers and sisters.

So when Bayard told the feechies about the impending invasion by the Pyrthens, there was really nothing more to talk about. Before night fell, a flotilla of flatboats had put out for the north edge of the swamp—a feechie army coming to the aid of their tribesmen.

The feechie warriors came by the thousands, across the black waters of the Feechiefen, through the scrub swamp, across the great pine savannah. They swam the River Tam, and in the moonlight their helmets looked like a horde of snapping turtles crossing the river into civilizer country. They came up the Overland Trail at a trot, and when they struck the River Road they turned north for Tambluff.

They arrived too late to save the capital city from the Pyrthens. But Bayard led the feechies on another two-day march to the south and west, toward the Clay Wastes. That was how the feechies came to be the heroes of the Battle of Sinking Canyons. New Vezey rose again that day, and the army of the great empire fell, swallowed up by the same ground that swallowed Corenwald's first village. That earlier catastrophe at Sinking Canyons sent the feechiefolk to the swamps and forests. Now another catastrophe, three centuries later, brought them back.

After a week of mourning for King Darrow and King Steren, the city of Tambluff devoted itself to a week of celebrations leading up to the crowning of Aidan Errolson as King of Corenwald. For now no one, not even Aidan himself, could deny that Aidan was the fulfillment of the Wilderking prophecy.

Tambluff had never seen such a week as that one. From every village in Corenwald people came to see the Wilderking crowned. That in itself would have filled the capital city beyond its capacity. But to that number the feechiefolk were added. All of them. Every he-feechie, she-feechie, and wee-feechie on the island crowded into Tambluff for the festivities. For the first time in three hundred years, there wasn't a human soul in the Feechiefen Swamp; it was given over to the alligators and craney-crows and bears and turtles for the week.

During the festival, the usual civilizer entertainments were augmented by such feechie pastimes as fire-jumping, gator-grabbling, and spitting contests. In the wrestling matches, feechies won every weight class except the heavyweights—and that was only because none of the feechies was big enough to qualify for the heavyweight class. The festive atmosphere was dampened somewhat by some grumbling among the civilizer wrestlers, who remarked on the feechie wrestlers' habit of biting their opponents and occasionally sticking their thumbs in their opponents' eyes.

Truth to tell, the grumbling wasn't limited to the civilizer wrestlers. There was more widespread grumbling about the nine alligators that high-spirited wee-feechies fetched from the moat of Tambluff Castle and turned loose in the city's High Street. And there was grumbling (and shrieking) on those unfortunate occasions when exuberant feechies dropped from shade trees into the fine carriages of civilizer ladies.

Taking it all around, however, the civilizers agreed that having feechiefolk in Tambluff was much better than having Pyrthens, so the protests were few. One of the most notable protests came from Lynwood and his family. When it came out that feechiefolk would be attending Aidan's coronation feast, Lynwood announced that he and his wife and daughters had socialized quite enough with feechiefolk and would miss the event.

Lynwood's daughter Sadie did, however, sneak off to the coronation feast, where she sat next to Dobro Turtlebane and shared a rotten lizard egg with him. Dobro and Sadie shared many more meals in the succeeding years, by the way. But that is another story.

The Pyrthens decided that their ambitions didn't extend to the island of Corenwald after all. That was just as well, for their army was in a weakened state after the disaster at Sinking Canyons. Besides, the Pyrthens had their hands full with a dozen rebellious subject states, which were now emboldened to fight against their masters.

Corenwald settled down to a long period of peace and prosperity under Aidan's kingship. That was a good thing, for the work of integrating feechie Corenwald and civilizer Corenwald into a single kingdom took every bit of King Aidan's wit and energy.

The day after the coronation ceremony, Brennus moved back to Longleaf Manor with his wife Gemma and their children and began reclaiming the family farm from the encroaching wilderness. Fershal of the Hill Country graciously gave up his claim to the land.

Maynard took a low-level position in his brother's government. Thanks to his steady work and his unswerving loyalty, he eventually worked his way up to the position of Corenwald's ambassador to the Pyrthen Empire.

Percy became Aidan's Secretary of State, and Jasper accepted a position at Tambluff University, where he immediately began his life's work: a seven-volume history of Corenwald, encompassing all of civilizer history and all of feechie history into a single narrative.

Dobro became Corenwald's Minister of Feechie Affairs, but that didn't stop him from sleeping in the treetops if he took the notion.

Bayard the Truthspeaker returned to his life of solitude in the forests and swamps, confident that his beloved Corenwald had been set to rights. Aidan hardly saw Bayard ever again. But he finally learned to take the old prophet's advice. He settled down to live the life that unfolded before him.

More about the acclaimed Wilderking Trilogy!

Book One:
The Bark of the Bog Owl
0-8054-3131-4

Book Two:
The Secret of the Swamp King
0-8054-3132-2

Book Three:
The Way of the Wilderking
0-8054-3133-0

"Portrays courage, faithfulness and friendship in a fantasy-adventure style akin to *The Chronicles of Narnia* and *The Lord of the Rings* . . ."
Christian Retailing

Jonathan Rogers calls The Wilderking Trilogy a fantasy-adventure story told in an American accent. The wild places of the imaginary island Corenwald bear more than a passing resemblance to the vine-tangled swamps and forests of his native Georgia. And in the voices of Corenwald's inhabitants— feechie and civilizer alike—you can hear the echoes of American swampers and frontiersmen.

Rogers holds a Ph.D. in seventeenth-century British literature from Vanderbilt University where he also taught English for five years. He lives with his wife and their six children in Nashville, Tennessee.

REALM OF
GORENWALD